THE FORBIDDEN LAND

OF

ANDARA

C.M RAYNE

THE FORBIDDEN LAND

OF

ANDARA

THE FIRST BOOK IN THE ANDARA SERIES

Adam Scythe drew the pictures

dancing paper

THE FORBIDDEN LAND OF ANDARA

Published by Dancing Paper
Cover art and illustrations by Adam Scythe
Constellation font by Marianela Grande

ISBN 978-963-12-1853-4

www.cmrayne.com

To my Viennese poppy

"Nothing in life is to be feared, it is only to be understood."

Marie Curie

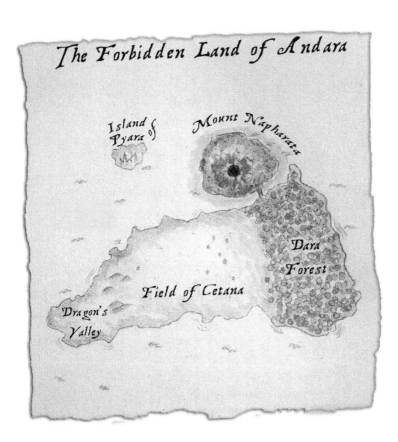

The Forbidden Land of Andara

Island of Pyara

Mount Napharata

Dara Forest

Field of Cetana

Dragon's Valley

1 THE WANDERING GIRL

Regina White didn't belong anywhere. At least that's what she often felt like. The outside world seemed desperate and cruel to her, so she chose to hide under a blanket in her cozy bed and run away to a world she considered to be better, whenever she had the chance.

After she got home from school, she spent most of her afternoons locked inside her bedroom, under the safety of her fuzzy blanket, reading a book. Preferably one far from reality. She didn't believe any of these worlds existed—in fact, she didn't believe in much at all. She just liked to take her mind off everything in the real world she didn't understand.

On a cloudy Sunday afternoon, Regina looked up from her book. She couldn't ignore the hunger in her stomach any longer. She placed her feet on the floor, took a deep breath and adjusted her eyes to the real world around her. She got up from her bed and set off for the kitchen. As she opened her bedroom door, she saw her mother standing in front of the mirror in the living room.

Sarah White was quite the sight. She was a middle-aged woman with thinning platinum blonde hair tangled up with cheap hair extensions, which failed to match the color of her own box dye job. A neon pink dress stretched across her enhanced breasts.

Regina was hoping she could step back into her bedroom without her mother noticing her presence, but she wasn't that lucky.

"Do you like this dress, Reg?"

Halfway back into her bedroom, Regina admitted defeat to herself regarding the mission of sliding back into her room unnoticed. She took a better look at her mother's dress, which looked too tight on her chest, too loose on the rest of her body and too inappropriate for her age. Too inappropriate for anybody's age, actually.

"Not really, Mom. That color is blinding," said Regina, admitting half of what she was thinking.

"You know I love this color, it's the color of life!" said Sarah, throwing her arms in the air, dramatically like she usually did.

"Okay, Mom. Wear what you like. You're very pretty." Regina gave in. "I just came for some food."

She felt sad for her mother, who was obsessed with her looks since Regina's father left the family for a young woman he had supposedly fallen in love with. Said woman was closer to Regina in age than to Sarah.

"Sure, honey, eat! There are some yummy things in the fridge," said Sarah as she tried to make her hair look more voluminous with her hands, but only managed to tangle the hair extensions even more.

Regina walked into the kitchen, which looked like it had not been cleaned since it was built. Brown spills of every shape and size decorated the tasteless yellow tiles and the tacky plastic tablecloth. The oven looked like it would catch on fire, if ever used, from all the built-up grease.

From the state of their home, one might have thought the White family was financially struggling, but they were actually well-off. Regina's father had left them a fortune when he decided to leave the family, in exchange for them never contacting him ever again. He wanted to start anew, and he couldn't allow his past weighing him down. Regina hadn't heard from him since the day he dragged his suitcases through the front door. He could have been dead for all she knew or living on a tropical island with a brand new family and children he was hopefully attached to more.

The gold accents of the French antique furniture he had left behind were now shining under a heavy layer of dust, so were the gold frames of the huge works of art on the walls.

Regina opened the fridge, which was probably white one day but had turned yellow over the years. Two diet chocolate bars and a moldy lemon stared back at her. With no better options available, she took one of the chocolate bars and went back to her room.

As she sat on her bed, munching on the chocolate, she felt a little sorry for herself. She was a hungry thirteen-year-old girl, and her mother couldn't care less about making her a decent meal or at least order one.

She knew her mother was unhappy. At least she didn't think someone who spends every week with a different man could be happy.

Sarah tried hard to lure a new man in, preferably a rich one, but for some reason no one stayed with her for long. At least Regina never saw one man twice.

Regina lay back on her bed and took another bite of the chocolate. She felt at ease in her room. No one or nothing could penetrate the warmth and safety of this space. Long black curtains kept the sun's rays out and allowed the warm fairy lights nailed all around the room to shine their light on the walls. The white sheets above her bed made the cozy corner look like a little fort, and the worn brown carpet in front of the red wardrobe never let Regina's feet get cold. This cozy little room made Regina feel safe no matter what was happening outside. Everything in this room felt like a part of her.

As she held the empty chocolate wrapper in her hand, she was not surprised by the fact that she was still hungry. She knew the other chocolate bar would not help the situation, and she was not desperate enough yet for the moldy lemon, so she decided to get her mind off her hunger by turning on the television.

"Three students were killed and six were wounded in a high school shooting today," announced the newscaster, her words piercing the comfortable space of Regina's room.

Regina quickly changed her mind about watching

television. She cut the newscaster off mid-sentence by turning off the television set so quickly that the remote almost fell out of her hands.

She had always had a hard time listening to the news. She couldn't understand why people did such things. Something inside her, though, desperately wanted to understand. Sometimes she even stayed up at night, searching for answers on the internet and reading about the minds of violent criminals. These long nights usually ended with panic attacks and zero hours of sleep.

Regina sat up on her bed when she realized she couldn't breathe. *This again.* She slowly steadied her breathing. She had experienced the choking grip of panic enough times to know what she had to do to calm down.

She took one last deep breath and decided not to deal with the human condition right now, so she lay back and immersed herself in her book again.

***

Regina was dreaming about a beautiful forest full of magical creatures hiding among the trees when a deep voice brought her back to reality.

"It's crazy how stupid people are," said the unnerving voice.

The clock on Regina's bedside table glowed with a bright four next to her brother, Tom, who was sitting on her bed, talking to her like he hadn't noticed she was sleeping. He was always very inconsiderate, but Regina honestly believed he wasn't like that on purpose, that he really didn't notice when a person was sleeping or didn't know that what he was saying was hurtful. She wanted to think that somewhere under his unfriendly attitude, he was a good person.

"Oh, were you sleeping?" Tom asked when he saw Regina rubbing her eyes.

"Yes," said Regina, a little annoyed. "Who's stupid?"

"You know, just this idiot who I sold my old phone to. He didn't even realize that he won't be able to turn it on tomorrow," he said with a proud smirk on his face.

"You sold that piece of junk to somebody? I thought you threw it out."

"I'm not going to throw out an item someone might pay for, are you serious?"

"Still, I don't think you should have done that," said Regina, not quite sure about her own opinion.

"Regina, seriously, you are so stupid. When I think I can talk to you, you always prove me wrong," said Tom with anger, like it was the most despicable act in the world to disagree with him.

He got up from the bed, took one last disappointed look at Regina, shook his head and left the room. As usual, he didn't close the door on his way out, so Regina stumbled across the room to close it. She didn't want to hear her brother's forceful voice telling their mother the same story, and her mother's proud reaction was also something she could have done without.

"Tom, you have business in your blood!" said their mother, hugging Tom.

Since she had failed to avoid this repulsive scene, Regina rolled her eyes and quietly closed her door. She couldn't help but think about her brother's words. Maybe she was stupid and didn't understand anything. Maybe his brother was a great businessman and would do great in life, and she was just a lost little girl who was not good at anything. Their mother was always so proud of Tom, whatever he did, but she was disinterested when it came to Regina.

Regina had a special look to her, even as a child. Her long ash brown hair and huge gray eyes almost sparkled in the dark, and her face always shone with a kind smile.

When she was little, her mother took her to child beauty pageants, but Regina's clumsy nature never won trophies. Her mother was so disappointed in her, she never showed interest in her endeavors after that. Regina questioned every choice she made, since no matter what she did, her mother couldn't have seemed less approving.

She looked around her room: at all the fairy lights that gave her comfort, the books that made her feel like she could be anyone. She felt childish and useless in that moment, and she wondered if she was actually like that.

Instead of wondering, she decided to do something no one could argue to be useful—her homework. She sat down at the table her late grandfather had left her. Before he died from complications from an injury he had suffered during war, he used to write short stories with Regina. He was a renowned author, who could make a person feel like they had traveled to the most magical places. He used to say wonder could be a better teacher than reality, and for some reason, this thought made Regina feel less tense every time it popped up in her head.

Regina smiled as she looked at the desk, and the memories of her grandfather swept through her mind like a warm embrace. She opened her math book with the same smile on her face.

***

She woke up the next morning with a book on her face. The alarm clock was screaming, and as she turned her tired head to look at it, she realized it had already been beeping for fifteen minutes. Regina was sure she was the only person in the world who continuously managed to oversleep with a working and quite loud alarm clock.

She stumbled out of bed and into the bathroom. Her eyes were sleepy, but they still sparkled with light. She didn't notice that though. She washed up and got herself together.

The television was turned on in the living room, and her mother was asleep on the couch. She always woke up around noon. Regina looked at her for a moment. She had fallen asleep with her makeup on again. The smeared eyeliner made her look like she had been crying. Regina wished her mother peaceful dreams, then she walked out the front door.

The sun was shining in the Renaissance apartment building's open stairwell. Regina took a deep breath of the cool morning air and set off for school. The city's busy streets were filled with people who were in a hurry to get to work or school, but Regina was an expert at making her way between them, since she had lived in the city all her life. She used her slim build to slide past people and reach school as quickly as possible, which usually took her a couple of minutes.

The private school Regina and her brother were attending was in a beautiful Gothic building. Its carefully crafted two towers pierced the bright sky. As Regina stepped into the building, she noticed the halls were empty. This was a usual sight for her, since it meant that classes had already started, and she was late for school almost every single day. She ran up the stairs. Her classroom was at the top of the right tower. She was so out of breath after climbing the stairs that she had to stop for a few seconds in front of the classroom before she entered.

"Excuse me, Professor Cropper," apologized Regina as she slid to her desk.

Professor Lyewar Cropper was a hefty man. Most of his face was hidden under his big curly auburn hair and beard, only his large green eyes were peeking out from under the hair-jungle. He was reading a poem for the class when Regina walked in, and it was common knowledge that the professor didn't like being interrupted. He took a scornful sideways glance at Regina, not willing to stop reading the poem.

"You picked a wrong time to be late," a playful whisper informed Regina.

The whisper came from Jasper Thorn, the thin boy sitting

next to Regina. His eyes shrunk behind his thick glasses as he smiled at her.

"Just when I thought Cropper couldn't hate me more," Regina said with a sigh as she quietly unpacked her books for the class.

Regina adored Professor Cropper. He was the school's English teacher, but he was also recognized in the literary world. The way he talked about literature astounded Regina from the very first class.

Professor Cropper, on the other hand, didn't show much liking towards Regina. She was always late and was too shy to contribute to the classes, so the professor thought she was just another uninterested student.

"The main theme of the novel is the darkness of man's heart. How the savage instinct, or the id according to Freud's theory, is still present in humans and always will be, even in the civilized world," said Jasper, sharing his thoughts with the class.

Regina admired Jasper's smarts. He was top of the class with seemingly no effort. Some teachers considered him a rare genius.

"Nerd . . ." whispered the blond boy sitting behind Jasper.

Regina turned around and gave him the dirtiest look she could squeeze out of her face.

There was no doubt that Pyro Marblestone had exquisite DNA. Every girl in the whole school would have given everything for a little shred of his attention. Some were even avid collectors of strands of his blond hair. He even enhanced his appeal by dressing like a typical bad boy—always in red and black, chains hanging from his distressed jeans. When he wasn't bullying Jasper, he was wearing large headphones on his head, blasting rock music into his ears. He didn't seem to enjoy anyone's company besides musclebrain Clive Wetwood's, who was a possibly even more unpleasant person than Pyro.

Pyro didn't look at Regina, he just smiled at his own remark smugly, like no one in the entire world existed besides him. It was often like that with Pyro. He didn't seem to care if he hurt others. It was just what he liked doing, so he did it without ever thinking twice.

Regina shook her head and turned back towards Jasper. She knew Pyro didn't care about her disapproval, she had expressed it several times before. Regina didn't understand why she seemed to be the only girl she knew who hadn't fallen for this guy. In Regina's eyes, he was more like a monster than a decent human being. She could easily imagine him turning into one of the criminals she had read about on the internet.

She smiled at Jasper. She always tried to be as nice as she possibly could to him. She knew how hard it was for the boy to endure the bullying he got every single day. It seemed to be taking a toll on him. It was not enough that he had to live with a father who seemed to be more interested in science than his own son since Jasper's mother died, Jasper also had to put up with the likes of Pyro.

21

"Class dismissed," said Professor Cropper ten minutes after the bell indicated the end of the class.

The halls of the school building came to life with the noises of students enjoying the little break they had between classes.

Jasper accompanied Regina to the school cafeteria, since Regina never had time to eat breakfast before school. Regina ordered two grilled cheese sandwiches, and the duo sat down on a wooden bench in front of their classroom. Regina began devouring her meal.

"I would say I don't understand how you can be so skinny while eating so much, but we both know I'd be lying," said Jasper, and Regina almost spat out her food from the outburst of laughter—she was happy when Jasper was comfortable enough to joke about himself.

As Regina tried to keep her breakfast in her mouth, a slender girl with long ice-blonde hair slammed into her back with a hug.

"Regina!" yelled the girl happily, hugging Regina tighter.

"Hi, Snow!" Regina squeezed her words out from beneath the surprisingly strong arms of the girl.

"I missed you so much! How was your weekend?" asked Snow as she twirled around Regina and sat on the floor in front of her.

"It was good. Yours?" asked Regina with a smile.

"It was really fun! We had such a great time in the park on Saturday, I was so sad you didn't come!"

"I'll go this week, I promise."

Regina loved Snow Gamy, her energetic but loving friend, who she knew since kindergarten. She was thirteen-years-old, like Regina, but she was in a different class. Snow was very outgoing and loved to spend time with a big group of friends from school. Regina accompanied them sometimes, but she enjoyed her alone time more.

"Pyro kind of said he likes me," said Snow, giggling into Regina's ear.

"Pyro? No! Wait . . . what? He doesn't even talk to people . . . Whatever, that's not the point! Come on Snow, you know what kind of person he is!" Regina snapped at Snow.

They all went silent. Jasper, who was still sitting next to Regina, pretended not to hear the conversation, since he was not friends with Snow. At the mention of Pyro's name he even looked in the opposite direction, like something truly interesting was happening there.

Snow glanced at Jasper apologetically for a moment, then she looked at Regina.

"I'm sorry," she whispered and stood up from the floor.

"Snow, you can't be serious." Regina stood up too to face her.

Snow stared at Regina in silence. Regina knew Snow liked Pyro, but she had always assumed it was only platonic, since she never actually saw them talk. She couldn't overlook the fact that Pyro was known for being the school bully, and that he had hurt so many people over the years, including Jasper. She just couldn't accept Snow, her childhood friend, in the company of such a monster.

"You just don't get him," said Snow in a dying voice then bit her lip and walked away from Regina.

Regina flopped down on the bench when Snow disappeared in the crowd.

"I don't get him . . . Please . . . Is she serious?" Regina turned towards Jasper, dumbfounded.

Jasper shrugged.

"She's in love," he said sarcastically and pulled a funny face.

Regina rolled her eyes and let out a little laugh, but as she turned her head back towards the crowd, she wondered if life would always remain this unfair.

***

Regina stayed in the school library after her classes to get her mind off Pyro Marblestone by reading some poetry. She decided it was time to go home when she noticed it was dark out. Her mother was not the worrying type, so she never had to inform her about her whereabouts. She never even noticed when Regina was not home anyway.

The city looked so different at this hour. Without hurry, it was still and calm. Regina walked slowly as she took in the peace of the city. She looked at the warm lights and wondered why life couldn't always be as simple and silent as it was in that moment. She stopped and looked at the few stars that were not dimmed by the bright lights of the city. She closed her eyes and took a deep breath, but before she could finish the inhale, her peace was broken by a strange noise coming from the dark alley behind her.

She turned around quickly and stared into the darkness of the alley. She couldn't see anything from the heavy blackness. The strange noise made itself heard again, but this time Regina could identify it—it was similar to the hooves of a horse against the hard concrete.

Regina was confused. What would a horse be doing in an alley? She began to worry the horse might have been lost somehow, so after deliberating the possible outcomes, her inner animal-lover won—she stepped into the darkness.

The alley was silent as she slowly made her way in. Her eyes slowly grew accustomed to the dark, and she could make out the old, blackened bricks of the walls.

Regina heard the sound again, but this time it was coming from next to her, the hooves slowly and deliberately placed right beside her—this was no horse. Her heart was beating in her throat. She was too scared to turn and look, but as she stared in front of herself, refusing to move, she realized her only choices were to look or to run away. Regina wanted to see.

She slowly turned her head, and the first thing she saw was a worn brown robe. Its inhabitant was about two feet taller than her, so Regina's fearful eyes were staring at a chest. Regina's shallow breathing sneaked the comforting smell of earth and flowers into her nose, and the scent somehow made her feel comfortable. She slowly lifted her head. The lights from the distant street shined on something that looked like goat horns, but Regina couldn't see the face of the creature until he lowered his head. The warm light shined on the kindest face of a man Regina had ever seen. Dirt brown dreadlocks framed his large brown eyes and a smile that exuded more peace than the calm city outside the alley.

The creature put one of his hands behind his back and softly put the other out towards Regina. His movements flowed like water.

All thoughts were gone from Regina's head. She had never felt this safe and at peace before. She reached out and placed her hand in the creature's warm palm. As the long fingers closed in on Regina's pale hand, she felt so at ease that she closed her eyes.

2. THE FIELD OF CETANA

Regina felt the bright sun warming her eyelids when she opened her eyes. The faun was still holding her hand, smiling.

"Welcome to Andara, Regina," he said softly.

When Regina adjusted her eyes to the brightness of the sun, she saw an endless vibrant green field before her. The soft breeze played with the grass and the small flowers all around the field. It was a place untouched by the hands of man. Regina stood in awe, admiring the beauty of the land.

She let go of the faun's hand and turned around. She was faced with a bright blue sea that seemed to merge with the infinite sky, on which millions of stars sparkled despite the fact that it was daytime. She took a deep breath, and the smell of clean air filled her lungs. The subtle waves of the sparkling sea made her feel like she had arrived home. Her eyelids were heavy with relaxation as she listened to the soft sound of the water.

"I can show you around if you wish." The kind voice surprised Regina—she had completely forgotten about the unusual creature.

She turned around to face him and was put at ease by the fact that the faun looked just as kind in the bright sunlight as he did in the dark alley. His long arms were placed behind his back as he patiently smiled at Regina.

Regina looked at the tall creature and the goat horns curling out from under his dreadlocks, and as she realized how absurdly sweet he looked, she smiled.

"Who are you, and where are we?" she asked.

"We are in the Forbidden Land of Andara, and I am your guide," replied the faun. "My name is Agnitio."

Regina opened her mouth to ask some more questions, but Agnitio didn't seem to need her to speak to know what she was thinking.

"Andara is a place every person visits at some point in their lives. You will meet many creatures here if you decide to stay. Creatures who can give you the answers you're searching for."

"So I can go back home anytime I want?" Regina asked, a little relieved.

"Of course, Regina. You are free to do anything you want. I should stress, however, that Andara is not a part of the world you came from, physically, but it is connected to it with a strong bond. Every choice made here defines that world as well. But I'll let the land answer your questions." Agnitio set off, and Regina followed. "By the way, time is non-existent here in Andara, so you don't have to worry about your life in the other world. You will continue where you left off when you go back," said Agnitio as they made their way through the seemingly endless field, which was an almost impossible shade of green. "This is the Field of Cetana. You will be starting your journey from here."

As they continued through the peaceful field, the silence of the land was broken by the faint sound of laughter. Regina began searching for the source of the sound, and she noticed a purple butterfly flying next to her.

"Is the butterfly laughing?" she asked.

"Yes, they are joyous creatures," said Agnitio as he put out his long index finger, and the butterfly took a rest on it. "Cute, isn't he?"

Regina took a closer look at the vibrant butterfly. Its unusually large eyes were on the end of its antennae. Regina could have sworn it was smiling at her.

"Interesting build for a butterfly," she said.

"He's different from how you're used to seeing them, isn't he? Nothing is as it seems, you will learn that here," said Agnitio and placed the butterfly on Regina's head.

As they continued their way through the field, a small hut appeared on the horizon. It even had its own little garden with vegetables and fruits.

"This is where I live," said Agnitio. "There are lots of similar huts all over the Field of Cetana, you will see. Come in, make yourself at home."

Regina stepped inside the hut, and the butterfly flew away with a faint laugh. The hut was a humble and warm home. It looked old, like it was the first home ever built, but homey and inviting nonetheless. There were wooden shelves all over the walls, filled with all kinds of items. An old plastic ball, a dried up flower, a strange rock, a piece of paper— they all seemed incredibly random. Regina sat down at the table as her eyes kept jumping from one object to another. She wasn't sure if it was impolite to ask about them, so she decided not to mention them.

"Tea?" the faun offered, picking up a cauldron.

"Sure, thank you," said Regina. "I really like your home."

"Thank you. It's not much, but it's all I need," said Agnitio as he poured Regina some tea.

Regina immediately smelled the enchanting scent of the liquid.

"What kind of tea is this? I've never smelled anything like it before," she said as Agnitio placed the cup of tea in front of her.

"It's made of an herb called Nangrass," Agnitio explained, taking a jar off one of the shelves. "This little guy is a Nangrass."

A fat root was sleeping in the jar. It looked like a peaceful little baby resting.

"Is it sleeping?" asked Regina, a pitch higher than usual.

"Yes. They are peaceful plants. They shed their skin in their sleep, that's what Nangrass tea is made of."

Regina took a sip of the crimson liquid. Its taste was not similar to anything she had ever tried before. It was, without a doubt, the most delicious beverage that had ever touched her tongue. On top of that, she could have sworn it made her more relaxed as well.

Agnitio put the Nangrass back on the shelf and sat down across the table from her.

"So, Regina, the creatures of Andara are all waiting to meet you."

"Me?" asked Regina with a slight squeal—she never liked attention.

"Don't worry, not just you," said the faun, smiling. "They await every human with open arms."

Regina nodded. She was a little embarrassed that she had thought, even for a second, that every creature in this world was waiting only for her.

"So, dear Regina, are you ready?"

Regina still didn't fully understand why she had been brought here, but she definitely didn't want to leave. The exciting promise of this new world got her interested. Plus, leaving her regular life behind for a little while was not a bad offer either.

"I think I am," she replied.

"I knew you would be," said Agnitio with a smile.

Regina felt at ease as she looked at the lovable creature.

"Regina, you should know that I'm always here. I can help you with whatever's troubling you, anytime, anywhere. You can choose to remember that if you wish," said Agnitio as he washed Regina's empty cup.

"I will remember. Thank you, Agnitio."

"I want to show you something," said Agnitio as he wiped his hands, then he opened the door for Regina. "Let's go."

Agnitio's hut stood next to a hill not too high but as wide as the eye could see. Agnitio made his way up the slope and Regina followed. When they reached the top, Regina was struck by the beauty of the view, but she couldn't lose herself in it for too long, because a giant roar broke the silence of the peaceful landscape. Regina immediately looked down in the direction of the sound, and she couldn't believe her eyes.

"Dragons?" she whispered.

"Yes, marvelous creatures," said Agnitio and sat on the ground. "This is Dragon's Valley."

Three large dragons inhabited the valley beneath them. A green, a brown and a black one. The green and the brown seemed peaceful as they lay in the grass, but the black one kept roaring.

"They are the masters of rebirth, therefor they are the masters of life," said Agnitio. "Saphira the Black is about to retire into her shell, that's why she's so tense right now. You see, dragons have the ability to be reborn when they think a change is in order. They form a cocoon, and once they come out, they are a new and improved version of themselves. They can develop new abilities, physical features or even personal traits."

Regina watched the black dragon curl up into a ball, and as it stayed in that position, a membranous scale layer started forming on its body until it covered the whole creature.

"What fortune you got to see this process! We got here

32

just at the right time."

"Are they dangerous?" Regina asked, sitting down next to Agnitio.

"If you have no reason to be afraid of them, they won't harm you. They are all-seeing. As they fly across the sky, they see the world as it really is. They can even see into one's soul. I believe they are similar to the creature Santa Claus in the other world, am I right?"

"Not really," said Regina, chuckling. "Santa Claus is not real. It's something made-up to entertain children."

"Is it? Or have you just lost your whimsy?" asked Agnitio, smiling.

Regina couldn't react to the speculation that Santa Clause was actually real, because she was poked in the back by something, which scared her so much that she almost rolled down the hill.

She turned around, and she was faced with a tiny black dragon. It was about eight inches tall as it stood on its four legs and flapped its wings. It had a strange scale formation on its face, which made it look like it had a bearded snout. As it looked at Regina with its big brown eyes, it sneezed, and a small flame blew out of its nose.

"I didn't know Saphira laid an egg," said Agnitio when he saw the small animal. "He seems to like you, Regina."

"Hello there," said Regina, greeting the dragon as she reached towards it.

The creature immediately rubbed his little face into Regina's palm and made his way towards her, flapping his wings. He climbed into Regina's lap, lay down comfortably and fell asleep immediately.

"I think it's decided," said Agnitio. "You will be his mommy until Saphira's being reborn. He can take care of himself, don't worry, he just wants your company."

The small dragon sighed in his sleep, which almost made Regina's pants catch on fire.

"Be careful with his fire breath though," said Agnitio, laughing. "They are not aware of it yet at this age. He doesn't know that one day he'll be one of the most aware creatures. Truly wondrous creatures, dragons. Would you like to give him a name?"

Regina looked at the tiny black dragon. He was growling in his sleep.

"How about Brunorth the Protector?"

"Perfect," said Agnitio, smiling. "We should go. It's getting dark."

Regina woke the tiny dragon up by gently placing him on the soft grass. They got up and climbed down the hill. Brunorth sleepily followed Regina like a shadow, stumbling on his little legs.

The sun slowly set, and the day's brightness gave way to the darkness of the night, but the stars were so bright that it was still easy to see everything. As they kept walking through the field, Regina soon noticed multiple huts appearing on the horizon.

"Who's living in these huts?" she asked.

"You'll see," replied Agnitio. "Do you see those two

huts? Which one would you like to stay in?"

One of the huts looked dilapidated to Regina, while the other seemed to be in better shape—a little run-down, but still cozy and inviting.

"That one doesn't look safe to me," she said, pointing at the dilapidated hut.

"Which one?" asked Agnitio, like it was not obvious which of the two huts looked like it could collapse any minute. "Oh, that one, I see." He nodded. "You would be surprised how many people think that's the safer choice."

"Really? How can that be?"

"Well . . . let's just say that in some way it is." When they arrived before the hut Regina had chosen, Agnitio said, "This is where I leave you, Regina. I suggest you rest. You start your journey tomorrow."

"Will I see you soon?" asked Regina, suddenly struck by the fear of being left alone in a place she didn't know.

"Of course you will. But remember that I'm always with you, even when you can't see me. There's no need for fear." Agnitio winked. "Good night."

The tall creature turned around and slowly disappeared in the now dark evening air. Regina stood in one place as she watched the kind creature's figure vanishing in the distance. As she listened to the fading sound of the friendly hooves against the soft grass, she felt the choke of panic slowly creeping in her throat.

Why was she here, required to explore this strange land? She felt the crippling crush of responsibility on her shoulders and suddenly began to doubt wanting to be here. It all seemed so complicated. Everything would be so much easier if she just went home and continued her life, forgetting she had ever been here.

"You can always choose to go back," said a whisper, breaking the night's silence.

Regina lifted her head.

"Who said that?" she asked.

"Come closer, child," the voice whispered.

Regina looked around and saw the blue flowers in the neighboring, dilapidated hut's little garden moving in the still air. She stepped closer to them and realized that they were the ones speaking.

"Yes, child, you don't have to be here. Just go home and forget about all of this. It would be so much easier. I remember your mother stood exactly where you're standing right now. She chose to forget she was ever here. Don't you want her to be proud of you? Just walk into this hut, and it will all be over."

The hut's old door opened with a loud creak behind the blue flowers. It looked worn—like it had been opened millions of times.

Regina's breathing was fast and shallow as she stared into the darkness of the decaying hut, and the voices of a million souls invited her to pass.

It would have been much easier to just forget about this whole experience, wouldn't it? To go home and continue her mundane life and be her mundane self. To go back to the familiar, to the secure. Who knows what she would be faced with here that she would never be able to forget.

As she stared into the inviting darkness, a teardrop rolled down her face. She didn't want to go back. She couldn't stand the thought of going back.

Even though the used doorway with the fingerprints of so many before her seemed like a safe choice, returning to her life was scarier to her than staying.

As the crippling weight of making a decision was eating her up inside, she felt a rush of enormous power break open inside of her.

"I want to stay!" she shouted into the beckoning blackness of the hut.

The old door immediately slammed shut, and the darkness of the night became silent once again.

Regina looked at the blue flowers, which were now still and showed no supernatural abilities. For the first time in her life, she felt she had made a good choice. She took a deep breath and combed through her long hair with her fingers, detangling the knots of the eventful day. As she looked up at the bright stars breaking through the darkness of the sky, she felt something she had never felt before—she was proud of herself.

When she turned around, she noticed Brunorth sitting before the other hut, tilting his head in confusion.

"Don't worry Brun, I'm not going anywhere," she said with a smile.

She went back to the hut she had chosen and petted the tiny dragon's head, who immediately turned on his back, exposing his belly. Regina laughed and sat down on the ground, next to her little friend.

"The stars are beautiful here. I'm glad you found me. We feel less alone together, right?"

Brunorth snorted in agreement.

"I'm a little scared, you know. But everything will be all right, won't it? We'll protect each other, little friend." Regina smiled at the dragon.

After a couple of minutes of looking at the stars, Regina

decided to take shelter from the cold of the night inside the hut, so she stepped inside in the company of Brunorth. She was amazed at what she saw inside. A climbing plant had grown all over the four walls of the hut. Dozens of small buds were hanging from the plant, and they shone like little warm stars. Their faint light lit up the whole hut. Regina smiled as she felt the warmth of her own room in the beauty of the tiny warm lights.

Brunorth climbed on the simple bed and curled up into a ball, ready to rest.

Regina opened the small wooden wardrobe next to the bed, and she was surprised to see it contained the same items as her wardrobe at home. She changed into her pajamas and lay down in the bed. The white covers were crispy and clean. She looked out the little window next to her. The stars flickered brightly through the darkness of the night. As Regina listened to the snore of her new friend and the sound of the distant sea, she drifted off to sleep among the guardian lights of the tiny buds, like a young flower awaiting the day to bloom.

3. FAMILIAR FACES

Regina woke up to the sound of Brunorth trying to climb up to the kitchen sink. The sun's bright rays caressed Regina's pale skin.

"Are you thirsty?" she asked, looking at the stumbling dragon. "Let me help you."

She got out of bed and sleepily walked to the little kitchen area in the corner of the hut. She opened a kitchen cupboard, which contained a couple of mugs, plates and cauldrons. She took out a wide mug, filled it with water and placed it on the floor, in front of the jumping dragon.

"Here you go."

Brunorth submerged his head in the mug as he devoured its contents.

Regina took another mug from the cupboard, which was shaped like a black dragon's head.

"Look Brunorth, he looks like you," said Regina with a smile as Brunorth continued to drink his water with such voracity, one might have thought he was on the edge of dehydration.

Regina filled the dragon's head mug with water and walked outside. The bright sun's unbiased rays felt warm against her skin. As she stood in the warm light, enjoying her mug of cool water, she suddenly heard the faint sound of laughter. Regina looked in the direction of the sound and saw three more huts not so far away.

She gave in to her curiosity and decided to look into the source of the laughter. As she made her way towards the huts, the sound started to ring familiar to her. She stepped over a little wooden fence and turned into the garden of the hut the noise was coming from. She couldn't have been more surprised to see Snow and Pyro lying among the flowers, laughing.

Regina's legs stiffened as she mutely stared at them. The image of the two of them being right there in Andara made her doubt her sanity for a moment.

"Regina? You're here too?" said Snow happily when she noticed Regina's presence and immediately jumped up to greet her friend. "Pyro and I were walking home from school when this strange creature basically appeared out of nowhere in front of us, and the next thing we knew was that we were here. How exciting, huh?"

"So you've met Agnitio too," said Regina with a sigh of relief as she came to the realization that she was not crazy.

"Yeah, he's such a cutie. There are a lot of other people here too. Pyro and I saw that there are a bunch of other huts here, and they are all inhabited."

"Hi Regina. Snow has told me a lot about you." Pyro got

up from the ground and reached towards Regina in hopes of a handshake.

Regina stared at him for a moment in confusion. Was he serious? After years of not even looking at Regina when she tried to protect Jasper, what in the world was he thinking?

"Yeah, hi," said Regina, giving the boy the cold shoulder and not shaking his hand.

Pyro scratched his head with the hand he had offered to Regina. Regina was surprised to see that the boy didn't seem smug at all—he seemed to be embarrassed.

Regina thought of what Agnitio had told her the other day: *Andara is a place every person visits during their lives.* All in all, she was glad to see familiar faces in this unfamiliar land, even if it meant putting up with Pyro Marblestone.

"I'm glad you're here," she smiled at Snow, who looked touched by Regina's confession.

"Are you really? Aren't you mad at me?"

"Of course not. You're my ancient friend, remember?" replied Regina as she playfully punched Snow's shoulder.

She honestly wasn't mad at Snow. At least for now, she had accepted that everyone, and that included her friend too, should be allowed to make their own decisions, no matter how horrible those decisions may seem. Regina was simply happy to see her friend.

"Do you guys want to check out the rest of the field?" Pyro suggested while flipping his shiny hair out of his face.

Regina still didn't sympathize with the conceited boy, but she didn't mind his presence at that moment.

"Sure," she replied.

"Let's go then!" Snow yelled as she hugged Regina and simultaneously pushed her out of the garden playfully.

As Snow and Regina laughed absent-mindedly, they heard a grunt from behind the hut.

"Brunorth!" exclaimed Regina. "I almost forgot about you!"

The tiny dragon was stumbling across the grass, towards Regina.

"Is that a dragon?" asked Pyro with excitement.

"And is it yours?" Snow added.

"He's not mine. We're just friends," replied Regina as she greeted her tiny friend.

"Really cool." Pyro nodded his head in appreciation.

Snow and Pyro both reached towards Brunorth, but the dragon started to growl malevolently at their approach.

"Okay, little buddy, you're the boss," said Pyro and took a few steps back from Brunorth.

Regina laughed at her vicious little friend and his accurate insight into character.

"We're exclusive friends, I guess," she said as she hugged Brunorth.

"So even mythical creatures like you, not just normal animals," said Snow with a smile. "You certainly have something about you that they are drawn to, I always envied that."

Regina jumped up from the dewy grass, surging with energy. "Okay, let's go then!"

Regina, Snow, Pyro and Brunorth set off towards the other huts.

"Have you met anyone other than Agnitio?" Regina asked Snow.

"I saw a weird-looking creature in the woods over there." Snow pointed to the forest that started to show up on the horizon. "It looked like a person, just longer somehow and with an all-black body. I couldn't make out what it was exactly. I asked Agnitio, but all he told me was that he's an important creature to meet. So we should go and check it out sometime. He looked really misshapen and creepy, but I might have seen him wrong."

"It sounds like he's the one we should be looking for," said Regina. "Or she."

"I think it was a he," said Snow. "I don't really know why. It just felt like a he for some reason."

As they got closer to the huts, it became clear that there were a lot of people there. They reached a small colony of huts where people were just standing around, talking. Everyone was around their age.

"Pyro!" yelled a deep voice. "What's up, bro?"

A tall, robust boy with short dark hair was approaching them. Regina recognized the obnoxious boy from school. It was Clive Wetwood. In some ways, he was even worse than Pyro in Regina's eyes. He was always the one laughing the hardest at Pyro's mean remarks, and he praised Pyro for his rude comments.

"So you guys are here too," he stated when he reached

the trio. "This place is super boring, dude. I think I'll step off soon."

"Yeah, it's really lame," replied Pyro with a change in attitude.

Regina noticed that the blond boy's voice had changed, even his posture was different since he noticed Clive.

Snow was standing in silence and looked uncomfortable.

"I'll take a walk around," Regina whispered to Snow. She had no intention of staying in the company of this gang.

"Come on, Brunorth," she whispered to the tiny dragon, who was growling at Clive from beneath the grass.

"See you later, Reg," said Snow quietly.

Regina and Brunorth walked away from the trio as Snow waved them goodbye. Regina didn't quite understand why Snow would choose the company of those two monkeys, but she didn't really care at this point, she just wanted to explore the land.

They made their way among the huts, looking at the different people.

"I really want to go home. I don't like this place," said one girl.

"I know. Me too. We should just leave," replied another.

"Are you guys talking about leaving? I want to go too." A third girl stuck her head out of a hut.

Regina didn't understand why anyone would want to leave Andara. It seemed like such a beautiful and intriguing place to her. Why would anyone want to go back to their everyday lives after seeing a place like this existed?

45

As she wondered, she noticed the three girls' bodies slowly fading away into nothingness. Regina rubbed her eyes to make sure it was not her vision playing tricks on her, but the girls were less and less visible, and after a few seconds, they disappeared completely.

From what she saw, Regina made the conclusion that the hut with blue flowers was not the only way back home—you could also return to your everyday life by simply wishing yourself back.

Regina turned around in search of Snow, Pyro and Clive. Since Clive wanted to leave, Regina thought he might have disappeared, but she was disappointed to see that the robust boy was still standing in the company of Snow and Pyro, laughing in his usual annoying sound.

"Was he lying?" Regina wondered.

Brunorth snorted in repugnance as he looked at Clive.

Regina looked around and realized that there were a lot less people around the huts than before. She felt sad about all these people leaving. The welcoming and kind face of Agnitio came to her mind and the disappointment he must have felt.

Regina decided to clear her head a little, so she made her way towards the seashore. After a couple of minutes of walking through the field, she and Brunorth reached the sea.

The sun sparkled on the calm waves. Regina lay down on her back and closed her eyes to enjoy the sound of the soft water.

***

She got so submerged in the relaxing sound that she didn't even know how much time had passed when she opened her eyes.

She didn't manage to keep her calm for too long, since a boy was sitting in front of her, drawing, and Regina got so startled by the unexpected presence of another human being that she immediately sat up in surprise.

"Oh, I'm sorry. Did I wake you?" the boy asked in a soft voice.

"I don't know. Was I sleeping?" Regina replied in confusion.

The boy laughed, and as Regina took a closer look at him, an entirely different feeling replaced her fright. The boy's raven-black hair sparkled in the sunlight as he quietly continued drawing. Regina was surprised to notice Brunorth sitting next to the boy, curiously looking at his drawing as the boy petted his head.

"Are you okay?" the boy asked Regina with concern. His large brown eyes were as warm as the sun as he looked at her.

"Sure, I'm fine," Regina answered quickly as she shook the fascinated expression off her face.

Regina had never seen a boy like him before, she had only read about them in books. A tall, cute boy quietly drawing on the seashore—he seemed just as rare of a creature as the half goat, half human Agnitio.

"Were you drawing me?" asked Regina.

"No, no," replied the boy and quickly closed his

notebook in an attempt to hide his drawing.

"You *were* drawing me! Can I see it?"

"It's not good," the boy replied, almost apologetically.

"I'm sure I'll like it. Please," Regina asked, and she sat next to the boy.

The boy looked into Regina's eyes for a moment, then he turned towards his notebook and gently opened it.

Regina was speechless. The soft strokes of the graphite formed an enchanted picture of a beautiful girl lying on the beach.

"I told you it's bad," said the boy and slammed the

notebook shut.

"No, it's beautiful. You are very talented."

"You're just saying that."

"I never say anything I don't mean. I really like it. Don't you?"

"I'm not sure," he said as he shrugged and gazed at the sea. The mixture of sadness and anger in his eyes gave the impression that he was discontent with much more than just a drawing.

"Well, it is truly wonderful, and I'm sad you don't see that. I mean, look at it!" Regina took the notebook from the boy and opened it to look at the drawing again.

"It's like the illustrations you see in books," she analyzed the picture deep in thought. "The soft water, the girl's smooth hair flowing in the wind, the sun sparkling on her skin—every little detail makes this picture so magical. You can see it was drawn from the heart when you look at it. Maybe that's why you're not sure if you like it—you're trying to make sense of something that can only be understood with the heart."

Regina was so mesmerized by the picture that she didn't even realize how unusual it was for her to share her thoughts with someone she had just met. It also took her a while to notice the silence. She turned to look at the boy, who was looking at her, smiling.

"I'm sorry, I didn't mean to intrude," she said self-consciously as she handed the notebook back to the boy. "I tend to overanalyze things. I'd better leave now."

She stood up, ready to leave in embarrassment, but when she heard the sound of paper tearing, she turned around. The boy tore the picture out of the notebook and was handing it to her.

"I would like you to have it," he said with the charming smile Regina was already familiar with.

"Thank you," said Regina and took the piece of paper. "Joey Herd," she added when she saw the freshly added signature on the bottom right corner of the paper. "Thank you, Joey Herd."

She smiled at Joey with a smile so big, it felt too big for her own face.

"Okay, I'll really be going now," she said and turned around to leave the situation, which felt way too awkward by now.

"I didn't catch your name," Joey remarked, to which Regina clumsily turned back again.

"I'm Regina. Regina White."

"Nice to meet you, Regina," said Joey.

"Nice to meet you too," she said, now calmed by the warm brown eyes of the boy. "I'll see you around. You're not planning on leaving, are you?"

"No, I think I'm staying." Joey nodded with a smile.

As Regina's eyes were jumping from his right eye to his left and back, she noticed how tired Joey's eyes looked. Looking at the boy sitting alone on the seashore filled her with the urge to give him a hug, but she resisted.

"Good," she nodded and turned around once more to

leave the beach for good this time.

As she and Brunorth were walking on the soft grass, she smiled to herself. She felt like she had made a new friend. She looked at the drawing in her hand—and that friend was someone special.

She cautiously turned around to take a peek at the boy. He was sitting in the same spot with his notebook in his lap, drawing. Regina smiled, but as she was sneaking a peek at Joey, a hand touched her shoulder like a sudden warning reminding her that it was not polite to stare.

"Jasper!" she exclaimed, her heart still violently beating in her chest. "You're here too! You're staying, right?"

"I am, I am. I'm very intrigued by this place," Jasper answered with a smile.

"Good," said Regina with a sigh of relief. "We can go exploring together!"

"Sure! We can start tomorrow."

"Tomorrow? Why not today?"

"Today? It's already getting dark. Look at these flowers." Jasper pointed at the small white flowers in the grass. "You can tell time by looking at them. Their petals close as nighttime approaches, and they open when morning is near. See? They're almost closed. Agnitio explained it to me. Interesting isn't it? They're called Fairypalms. I suppose you've met Agnitio too."

"Yes, I most definitely did," said Regina with a smile. "He gave me Nangrass tea."

"Tea? I didn't get tea," complained Jasper.

"You only missed out on the best-tasting tea ever," teased Regina as she playfully put her arm around her friend. "Show me your hut!"

Jasper led her to his hut, which looked the same as Regina's and Agnitio's. They sat down at the table when Regina's stomach suddenly made itself heard with a violent growl.

"I didn't even eat anything today, I totally forgot," said Regina, looking at her noisy tummy.

"Did you take a look in the kitchen cupboards?" Jasper asked.

"I found mugs, plates and cauldrons in one."

"You didn't look in the others? They're full of food." Jasper opened the cupboards to show their contents to Regina. They were filled with rows of bottles and jars, all containing various fruits, vegetables and herbs.

"What are these?" Regina asked as she approached the cupboards to take a closer look at them. All the jars and bottles were labeled, but the names written on them were not familiar to her. "G'moraash, Feldurarice, Adderblue, Drexlorash," Regina read the labels aloud. "Seriously, what are these?"

"I'm not sure, but I assume they are all edible, otherwise they would not be here." Jasper pulled a jar out of one of the cupboards. It contained a bright blue, leafy vegetable-looking plant. "Rainlettuce," he read the label then opened the jar and smelled the plant. "That's unexpected. It smells sweet."

Regina smelled the strange plant as well. Her stomach growled as she inhaled the sweet scent, and she realized how hungry she was. "Oh, that smells good. Let's eat it!"

Jasper laughed at his friend's voracity and pulled out the plant from the jar. Its dewy leaves opened as he washed it.

"Here," he said, tearing off a leaf and giving it to Regina.

"Thank you," said Regina and stuffed the unusually large leaf into her mouth.

The taste was just as good as the scent. The sweetness filled Regina's mouth, and as she swallowed the tasty bite, she realized that the plant was surprisingly satisfying. After eating only one leaf each, they both felt full.

Regina found a jar in the cupboard, labeled *Nangrass*, so they boiled some water and made tea. They sat in front of the hut with the warm beverages in their hands.

"Regina, I don't want to scare you, but there's something in the grass in front of you," whispered Jasper.

"Oh, that's just Brunorth," said Regina with a sigh of relief. "I forgot to introduce you two to each other. Brunorth, meet my friend Jasper. Jasper, this is Brunorth."

"Is he a dragon? How magnificent."

"Yes, they live behind the hill, in Dragon's Valley. Her mother is being reborn right now, so we became friends."

Brunorth waddled to Jasper and sniffed his legs, but when Jasper tried to pet his head, the tiny dragon growled as a warning.

"He has not been very friendly with most people."

"He's truly astounding," said Jasper, amazed.

"Are you looking forward to being here?" asked Regina.

"Very much. This seems like an extraordinary place. I'm assuming that all the incompetent people will disappear shortly, making this an experience for the truly deserving."

"I'm surprised at how many people choose to disappear from here. I mean, aren't they even interested?"

"Change scares people. They would rather go back to what they already know, what they view as secure, even if the new might be better."

As they were talking, the backdrop of the stars changed from light blue to black.

"I think I'll turn in." Jasper yawned. "We'll explore the forest tomorrow, right?"

"Sure, I can't wait. I'll let you rest then. Good night."

Regina waved goodbye to her friend and made her way back to her hut with Brunorth. She took a shower in the hut's small bathroom and curled up with the tiny dragon in the comfortable bed. As she lay in the warm light of the plant's buds and the stars, she thought of the eventful day she had had. She had met up with Snow, Pyro, Clive, Jasper and even made a new friend—Joey. She had probably been asleep for a long time on the beach, but she'd make up for the lost time tomorrow.

She hadn't even journeyed to a new place yet, but she had already experienced so much. She saw the people she knew in a new light here, and the people, creatures and plants she had gotten to know here all seemed magical and wonderful. Her heart filled with warmth as she thought of the

Forbidden Land of Andara. There was nothing scary or saddening in this place. Not even the all-black, misshapen creature lurking in the woods seemed scary to her in that moment.

4. THE GUARDIANS OF DARA FOREST

As the sun rose the next day, the morning was bright and warm again. Regina and Brunorth tried a fruit-looking plant for breakfast, which Regina found in one of the kitchen cupboards, in a jar labeled *Adderblue*. It was just as tasty and fulfilling as the Rainlettuce. After eating breakfast, Regina and her tiny dragon friend met up with Jasper, and they set off for the forest.

"What do you think we'll find in there?" Regina asked Jasper.

"I'm not entirely sure, but whatever is in there, I'm sure it will be intriguing."

"Snow said she saw a strange creature in the woods."

"Please spare me the delusions of your friend. I wish to explore this place without the non-sense of our life back home."

"I'm sorry . . ."

It was not rare for Jasper to snap at Regina for simply mentioning something that had the slightest connection to Pyro or Clive. Regina never mentioned this to Jasper, because she knew her friend was going through a hard time.

Jasper had been a victim of bullying all his life. He and Regina even became friends when she once interfered and defended him against Pyro and Clive. She felt an obligation to be the best friend she could be to Jasper, since she was the only one.

"I think that's the creature we should be looking for in there though," said Regina, as nonchalantly as she could. "He's some kind of black and misshapen-looking creature supposedly."

"Black, misshapen. Got it. He sounds like he'll be hard to miss." Jasper's voice rang with annoyance.

Regina loved Jasper very much, but sometimes she felt like the rage Jasper felt as a consequence of all the bullying took over him, and it could bury his loving personality somewhere deep inside him. When this happened, Regina quickly changed the subject and didn't give up until Jasper was back to his loving self. Distracting him with an interesting scientific topic seemed to do the trick most of the time.

"Look! What an interesting bug!" Regina exclaimed and crouched down on the grass.

"It looks like an ordinary stag-beetle," said Jasper as he examined it, "so it's actually an insect, not a bug. All bugs are insects, but not all insects are bugs, you know."

"We're in Andara. I'm sure it's neither bug nor insect."

As the creature opened its wings, its abdomen became visible underneath, which paraded in all the colors of the rainbow.

"Nothing's really as it seems here, is it?" said Regina with a smile as the colorful creature flew away.

"It goes against all the natural rules of survival." Jasper watched it disappear in awe.

"This is not a place for rules." Regina gently nudged Jasper towards the forest, being proud of herself that her plan to distract Jasper had worked.

The forest shaded them from the rays of the sun as they stepped among the trees. The field's brightness changed into dewy shade. All the trees were tall and looked old; like they were standing right there since the beginning of time.

"I don't think I've ever seen trees this big," said Regina. "They are beautiful."

"Thank you for your kindness," replied a deep voice that sounded like an old man's.

"Did you say that?" Regina asked Jasper.

"No, I most certainly did not say that," Jasper replied.

They searched for the source of the voice, but they didn't see anyone nearby.

"Can't see the forest from the trees?" The old man's voice laughed. "Don't just look, child, see."

Regina stopped turning in search of the voice and looked straight ahead, right at the trunk of the old tree in front of her. The bark cracked open and formed a human-like face. A horizontal slit curved upwards, making it look like the tree was smiling.

"You see? Sometimes all you have to do is stop," said the

old tree. "My name is Lagurus, and I welcome you to Dara Forest."

"Are you talking?" Regina doubted her own eyes.

"Yes, I am," said the tree.

"But . . . you're a tree," said Jasper.

"What's your point? That you are so fixed in your views that you can't even accept what's before your own eyes? You need to shed that attitude now, if you wish to continue your journey through Andara."

Regina and Jasper looked at each other.

"Just one thing, dear children," said the old tree. "Be wary of the creature in black who once called himself human. You would be surprised how easy it is for him to fool you."

"The creature in black? That must be the one we're looking for," said Regina. "Should we avoid him?"

"I didn't say avoid. I said be wary. Now please leave me. Autumn is approaching. I need to prepare myself."

Regina and Jasper nodded and turned around, leaving the tree behind and continuing their way through the forest.

"What do you think he meant?" asked Regina when they were far enough from the tree.

"He said that this creature once called himself human," answered Jasper. "I can't imagine what that might mean. But I'm sure we'll find out soon."

"Did you hear that?" Regina froze in her step when she heard a strange noise coming from the depth of the woods.

"I think someone's singing," said Jasper.

"Could it be the once-human?"

"It's a voice of a female, so I don't think so."

"It's coming from over there," said Regina, pointing at a suspicious bunch of trees.

They sneaked closer to the trees, which were unusually close to each other, and as they approached, the song became more and more understandable. They heard the soft voice of what sounded like a little girl:

Little sparkles, don't you fear
All is done, the end's not near
The forest's waiting for your cheer
I am here for you, my dear.

Regina peeked between two trees. Bright lights shining in every color of the rainbow dazzled her eyes. The sources of the lights appeared to be small orbs floating around a girl who was sitting in the middle of a small circular field, which was surrounded by tightly grown trees.

The girl's white hair was so long, it covered the ground around her. It was also wrapped around a large piece of branch in front of her, and she was using this contraption as a harp—she was playing a soft melody on her own hair.

The different-colored orbs seemed to enjoy the girl's song. As they floated around her, they appeared to be dancing.

Regina and Jasper stared at the scene amazed, listening to her song as well, but the girl suddenly stopped singing, and the orbs stopped their joyous dance too. She remained motionless for a short while, but then she suddenly jumped up and began pacing on the perimeter of the field, looking at the surrounding trees. The branch was still tangled in her hair, which she just dragged behind herself on the ground, and the colorful orbs followed her every move.

"Where did she go?" asked Regina when the girl disappeared from her field of vision.

She got her answer immediately, when the girl jumped in front of her, staring between the two trees, at Regina. Her hair covered her face, but her large bright purple eyes could still peek through. The color of her eyes matched the purple, sack-like dress she was wearing, and her bare toes wiggled in excitement as she stared at Regina.

"I see you too," said the girl, pointing at Jasper, who was trying to take a step back from the trees. Her voice was soft, high and calm, and even though she was now talking, her voice still sounded song-like.

"I'm sorry we disturbed your beautiful song," apologized Regina—she didn't dare move while the girl was staring at her.

"You didn't disturb my song, no need to apologize," said the girl, closing her large eyes and giving a sweet smile to Regina. "What are you waiting for? Come in! Come in!" she said and pulled Regina through the narrow gap between the trees. "You too!" She turned towards Jasper and pulled him into the circular field as well. "Oh, a baby dragon," she said when she saw Brunorth stumbling through the trees. "Wondrous creature, you will grow up to be, little soul." She gently petted his head, which Brunorth seemed to deeply

61

enjoy.

The short girl now turned to Regina and Jasper. She bowed her head and gave a curtsey. Regina noticed that she, too, had horns on the top of her head, but hers looked more like the antlers of a deer, and they weren't as visible as Agnitio's because of her great amount of hair.

"I am Y'sis, Guardian of Souls. Nice to meet you Regina and Jasper, wanderers of Andara." Y'sis smiled as she straightened up. "This is the Circle of Jivana. I guess I spend most of my time here. You see, Andara is a place where you can come while you live, and also after you die. Just not as a human anymore, of course." Y'sis' voice rang with an otherworldly tone that felt like sweet caresses to the ears. She put out her palm, and the green orb descended onto it. "I'm here to soothe the fear of the newcomers who descend from the sky. It's scary to lose your worldly shell, you know. But fear is not of use here—that's what I help them understand. After all, their lives only just start here." Y'sis smiled, and she seemed moved as she looked at the bright pistachio green orb.

Regina smiled too as she looked at the small girl. The gentle love Y'sis had in her eyes for her orbs made Regina feel warm inside.

"I guess you're not the once-human dressed in black."

"The who?" asked Y'sis, snapping out of her mesmerized state. "Oh, you mean Eris."

"Eris?" Regina's inquiry didn't result in answers, because Y'sis' attention was grabbed by a grunt coming from the other side of the tightly grown circle of trees. It sounded like an old man mumbling in anger.

"That's Heathcliff," explained Y'sis. "You must have stepped on a flower."

63

Y'sis slid out between two trees, and Regina and Jasper followed. A small creature was crouching in the grass. He looked like a small, enchanted repairman. He had a utility belt full of what seemed like different potions.

He picked out one of the bottles from his belt and poured a few drops of its contents on a crushed flower. The flower absorbed the drops and immediately straightened up and opened its petals. It suddenly looked like it had never been crushed.

The creature stood up and toddled out of the area, walking by the trio but giving them no mind, still angrily mumbling.

"Good day, Heathcliff," Y'sis greeted him.

The creature stopped, looked at Y'sis and nodded his head then continued on his way. Y'sis continued to smile at him until he disappeared among the trees of the forest.

"That was Heathcliff. He's an elf," she explained. "They might seem unpleasant, but they're quite the wonderful creatures. They are nature's guardians, you see. They help those who can't help themselves."

Y'sis stared at the healed flower, lost for words. It was clear by now that she was easily mesmerized.

"Regina and Jasper," she said, turning towards them with her purple eyes wide open, "I can only offer guidance to live humans if they have rare souls. Like white or black for example. Your souls are extraordinarily average."

Regina and Jasper looked at each other.

"Oh, that's quite fortunate, actually," said Y'sis. "Rare

souls can be troublesome to live with. They are heavy to carry, so to say." She seemed to fall deep into thought about the hardships of those with rare souls for a couple of seconds. "Well, I'd better get back to my job," she said abruptly, startling Regina and Jasper. "My little friends are starting to get agitated. I understand you're looking for Eris. You will find him if you continue straight ahead." Y'sis began walking back to her field. "Don't let him get into your head though. He has a knack for trouble. He manages to get to people more often than I care to think about." Y'sis shook her head, and the concern that appeared on her face worried Regina. "Well, farewell Regina and Jasper, and don't forget: when in doubt, look at the stars."

Y'sis disappeared behind the trees, and Regina and Jasper heard the sound of her song again.

"Eris," said Regina. "That's who we're looking for. He's the once-human in black. He doesn't sound too pleasant, does he?"

"He certainly does not." Jasper took a deep breath then looked at Regina. "I'm intrigued," he said with a twinkle in his eye.

Regina laughed, put at ease by her friend's excitement.

"He can't be that bad, we're in Andara," she said, winking at Jasper.

They smiled at each other then set off in the direction Y'sis had suggested.

They continued deeper into the forest and went on for hours, seeing nothing or no one out of the ordinary. They simply enjoyed the beautiful trees and greeted the occasional speaking ones.

"We should stop and rest for a little," suggested Jasper, rubbing his legs in pain.

"Great idea," replied Regina, and she plopped down onto the ground to stretch out on the grass.

"I prepared some food for us," said Jasper and sat down next to Regina.

"I didn't even think of that! I'm glad you're here, you know?" Regina sat up to take a look at the large bowl Jasper pulled out of his backpack. "What is that?"

"I made a salad. I don't know what these plants taste like exactly, but I hope their flavors complement each other."

Jasper sitting in the grass with his bowl of carefully prepared food made Regina smile. The boy she saw in that moment was the kind and caring friend she loved so much.

"I'm sure it tastes amazing, you can do no wrong," she said, putting her fingers in the bowl to grab some of the salad.

She put the handful of food, which was as bright and vivid as a rainbow, in her mouth, and an unusual flavor filled her mouth. It was not quite sweet, not quite sour and not quite salty, but rather all of those flavors at the same time, and the most surprising fact was that it didn't taste bad—it tasted amazing.

Jasper and Regina nodded at each other in fascination with the Andara plant salad. Regina gave a handful to Brunorth as well, who was curled up in the grass, next to

66

her. He seemed to enjoy the salad too, which he voiced with a fiery burp.

"That looks really good," said a familiar voice coming from behind them.

Regina turned her head, and she felt her heart pound against her chest when she saw Joey.

"Hi Joey! Nice to see you!" Regina tried her best to seem calm, but she felt like she was failing terribly. "This is my friend, Jasper."

"Hello Jasper. That's a tasty-looking salad you got there," said Joey as he shook hands with Jasper.

"Nice to meet you," said Jasper. "You are more than welcome to have some," he added and offered the bowl to Joey.

"Thanks, I'm really hungry." Joey took a handful of the bowl's contents and stuffed it into his mouth. "I'm being really rude, aren't I?" he asked with his mouth full and cheeks turned red.

"No, it's fine," said Jasper with a laugh. "How do you two know each other?"

"We just met yesterday," answered Regina, who was also smiling at Joey's embarrassment, which she actually found adorable.

"Oh, I see. You're welcome to join us if you'd like."

"Thank you, that would be great. Everyone I know chose to go back home. Not that I have that many friends to begin with, but . . . you know."

Joey sat down next to them. Brunorth seemed happy to

see him as he looked at him and contentedly acknowledged his presence. The trio ate the rest of the salad together.

"So, where are you from?" asked Jasper.

"I'm from the fifth district of Tupsbade."

"I'm from the seventh!" exclaimed the surprised Regina. "We live really close, what a small world."

"I live in the second, if anyone's interested," said Jasper.

"That's really cool, we all live in the same city," said Joey with a smile. "So, where are you guys headed?"

"Y'sis told us to come this way, so we just came this way. We don't really know where we're going," explained Regina.

"Oh, Y'sis was so cute, I met her too. She asked me to draw on her arms with some kind of natural body paint or something. I thought it was temporary, but she told me after I'd finished that it was actually permanent. I'm glad she liked what I drew on her."

"Permanent, really? What did you draw?" asked Regina.

"I'm not really sure. They ended up like some kind of strange signs, but I didn't really think about it, I just drew what came naturally, since that's what she specifically asked me to do. It ended up looking cool though, and she seemed really happy with it, so that's what matters."

Regina slipped her hand inside her pocket, in which she kept the drawing Joey had given her on the beach the other day. She felt strangely attached to the picture and wanted to make sure that she didn't lose it.

"When did you arrive in Andara?" she asked.

"A few days ago. On the twentieth, at 9:43 pm, actually."

"How come you remember the exact minute?" asked Regina.

"I remember because I had a little fight with my parents," Joey explained then kept quiet for a moment. "I actually slept on the street that day. Next to the big clock on Grape Street that displays the date and time. That's where I met Agnitio. So that's why I remember it."

No one said anything for a few seconds. Joey began playing with the grass in front of him, so he didn't have to look at Regina or Jasper. Regina was the one to break the uncomfortable silence.

"We've all been there," she said as encouragingly as she could, but the words didn't come out as she had hoped.

"You've also slept on the street before because your parents threw you out?" Joey asked with a half-smile.

"No, but I've slept on the street before when I was seven years old, because I didn't find my way back home from school."

The two boys burst out laughing.

"Did you really?" asked Jasper when his laughing calmed down enough to muster out the words.

"Yes, I really did. The police found me on a bench in the middle of the night and took me home though."

"I can still so imagine you doing something like that," said Jasper still shaking from laughter.

"Yes, I would still totally do it. It's a better choice than wandering around the city all night," said Regina, now also laughing.

Joey gave a thankful smile to Regina. Regina felt comfortable in the company of the two boys. She was happy in that moment. Laughing at the frivolity of life with her friends and a full belly—everything seemed so easy. They talked and joked around for a few hours there, in the middle of the calm forest. When they felt rested and full of energy again, they decided to continue on their way together.

"This just keeps getting better. I might never want to leave," said Jasper.

"I'm having a really good time too," replied Regina as they made their way through a particularly tall and spiky bush. "But there has to be something at least mildly unpleasant here. Like the once-human in black."

"The who?" asked Joey.

"Didn't you hear about him? Supposedly, he's who we should be looking for," said Regina.

"I just came into this forest because I like forests," admitted Joey. "I didn't even think about searching for someone."

As they stepped out from among the thorny branches, a huge pitch black castle unfolded before their eyes. Its sharp, unwelcoming towers pierced through the sheltering crowns of the trees like merciless spears.

"But then again, I probably should have." Joey's careless expression turned stunned, just like Regina's and Jasper's.

They stood in silence and stared at the dark building that towered over them like a synthetic beast in the ancient forest.

5: THE BLACK CASTLE

The castle looked like it was built from black marble, it was such a deep and shiny black. It was as intimidating as a building could be, and it didn't help its unfriendliness that it didn't appear to have any windows. It stuck out like a sore thumb in the peaceful forest.

"I would advise against going in there," said Jasper, his previous excitement nowhere to be found.

"Are you kidding? This is probably where the once-human is," said Regina. "And Y'sis told us to come here too."

"I mean, it's what we're here to do, isn't it?" said Joey. "What's the worst that could happen?"

"Are you kidding?" asked Jasper. "May I remind you that we are in a strange land, surrounded by strange creatures? Just a few hours ago, we met a little girl who probably welcomed the dead. So, the worst that could happen is that we fly back to Y'sis as shiny little orbs."

"Wow, you're enthusiasm ran out quickly," said Regina.

Joey walked closer to the castle and touched its shiny

black wall.

"You guys," he said, his voice suddenly serious, "you have to see this."

Regina and Jasper approached the building. When they reached its wall, Regina looked at her reflection in the glossy material. The dark wall did not reflect reality. The person she saw was not the same person who usually looked back at her from a mirror. This woman was old, and the malicious wrinkles on her face told the story of a life lived in fear and anger. She looked at Regina with eyes filled with resentment.

"Who are you?" Regina asked, fearing the answer.

The old woman looked her up and down with disgust.

"I am who you might become," she whispered. She spat her words like they were bitter in her mouth.

Regina shook her head and stepped back from the wall. She tripped on her own feet and fell back. When she looked at the wall from the ground, the woman was already gone.

"Are you okay?" asked Joey and rushed to help Regina up.

"I'm fine," she replied in a dying voice. "Jasper?"

Jasper was motionless as he stood staring at the wall.

"Jasper, dude, are you okay?" Joey approached him with caution.

Jasper continued to stare at the dark wall without blinking. He was shaking. Joey put his hand on his shoulder, and Jasper immediately looked at him, like he was caught in the middle of something he shouldn't have been doing.

"It's okay," Jasper said, sputtering his words. "I'm okay.

It will be okay." He seemed to be trying to convince himself rather than Joey.

"Everything's fine. Breathe," said Joey, still keeping his hand on Jasper's shoulder.

"What did you see, Jasper?" Regina asked, struggling to form the words with her trembling lips.

"Nothing," Jasper replied, still shaking. "Just my reflection, you know."

Regina felt her eyes well up, but the crippling feeling radiating from her stomach to every other part of her body scared her so much that crying lost its priority. The images in her head were too much to keep up with. Her future as the dreadful old woman, Jasper's probably just as horrible future, their journey across this unknown land, the uncertainty of it all . . . She couldn't breathe. *This again.* On top of everything, she couldn't even breathe. She wanted to smash the dark castle that had destroyed the last thing she believed in.

"It's okay."

"Calm down, Regina, everything's fine."

Both Jasper and Joey rushed to Regina, who was now crouching on the ground. Brunorth was looking at her with concern, turning his little head left and right in confusion.

Regina tried to steady her breathing, which was not so easy this time.

"It's all right," said Jasper, putting aside his own issue to soothe Regina. "Stabilize your breathing. Inhale to the count of five and exhale to the count of seven. You know the drill."

Regina's eyes welled up with tears again, but this time because of the selflessness of her friend. Jasper smiled at her and encouragingly nodded while she kept on breathing as he instructed. Regina felt her body and mind settle down like the violent waves of the sea becoming calm. It was easier to breathe again.

Brunorth tried to help out by licking Regina's hand, which resulted in a mild burn.

"Ouch." Regina sniffled and let out a little laugh. "Thank you, guys. I'm fine. I'm so sorry. I don't know what got over me. I guess I don't handle new experiences very well."

"It's okay, we're all in this together," said Joey with a smile.

Regina felt bad as she looked at the two boys smiling at her. They had both gone through the same thing, and neither of them had great lives back home, but they could still contain themselves. Why couldn't she ever contain herself? She felt so foolish, but decided to pull herself together and not be a burden to the boys anymore, so she wiped the tears from her face and got up from the ground.

"So, are we going in?" she asked, smiling as she took a fresh, new breath.

The two boys looked at each other and nodded.

"Yeah, let's go," said Jasper. "It will be fine."

The trio made its way up the long marble staircase, which led up to the entrance and was just as pitch black as the rest of the castle. As Regina climbed the stairs, she was a little worried about what they might have to face inside, when even the outside of the walls were this distressing.

When they reached the top of the stairs, they were faced with a large black wooden door. The door had different symbols carved into it, and in the middle, large letters displayed the words *HOSTIS HUMANI GENERIS*.

"Enemy of the human race," said Jasper, examining the door.

"Excuse me?" asked Regina.

"It's in Latin. Hostis humani generis," Jasper explained as

he traced the carving with his fingers. "It means enemy of the human race."

"Friendly," said Joey.

Regina took a deep breath, trying to remain collected. She was still far from being calm.

"Do you know any of these symbols?" she asked Jasper.

"It looks like the ancient scripts from Mesopotamia."

"Mesopotamia?" Regina gathered her brows. "How old is this place?"

"Very." Jasper was still tracing the carvings on the door with his fingers, looking a lot like an archeologist.

Regina and Joey stood staring at the large door, and Regina wondered what a once-human might be like. Her thoughts about the creature in black didn't help soothe her anxiety, so she took another rushed deep breath and said, "Let's just knock." She pointed at the large iron knocker right under the Latin words.

Joey lifted the large knocker, which was about ten times as big as an average one. He pushed it up with the help of both his arms, and after he lifted it, he just let it fall back down as he avoided the impact. The iron ring made such a loud noise that they had to cover their ears. As the noise faded away, the large door slowly opened, giving forth a long squeak, but no one appeared to be on the other side.

"Hello?" said Regina, her voice echoing in the darkness.

"Is anybody there?" Jasper added.

No one answered and nothing happened. Only the dark hall's cool air crept up to their faces.

"Can we come in?" asked Joey, to which they finally got an answer in the form of lights turning on, lighting up a huge hall filled with hundreds, if not thousands, of books.

"Is that a yes?" said Joey, looking at Regina and Jasper.

Brunorth got fed up with their hesitation, so he marched in the large hall.

"Brunorth! Wait! No!" Regina yelled, but the tiny dragon didn't listen to her. "Oh, man. I guess we have to go in now."

The trio carefully stepped into the cold hall. The floor was just as black as the exterior of the castle, but the walls were not visible here, since they were filled with books from the ground to the ceiling. A large staircase, which was a smaller version of the one outside, led up to a hole in the ceiling. The source of light was the same kind of shining plant that could be found in their huts. It grew all over the ceiling, and its buds were hanging down like little light bulbs.

"I didn't know Andarians read books," said Regina as she took a look at one of the shelves. "*Nine Books of Disciplines, The Emperor's Mirror, Suda, Lexicon Technicum, Wakan Sansai Zue.*" She read aloud the titles of some books that had somewhat comprehensible titles—a lot of them were written in languages Regina couldn't even recognize. "What are these books? I've never heard of them."

"They are historical encyclopedias," said Jasper, examining them. "All of the historical encyclopedias ever written, it seems."

"Whoever lives here must be the most educated creature

ever," said Joey.

"Andarians didn't seem interested in the kind of knowledge books can provide, Regina is right." Jasper was thinking aloud. "This collection had to come from our world."

"Do you think . . . ?"

Regina's question was interrupted by a sudden noise, which seemed to be coming from the hole in the ceiling.

"Woah, okay, what was that?" Regina began feeling a bit unwelcome. "Should we go?"

"Yes, but not back. I think we should go up," said Joey.

"I agree." Jasper had already made his way towards the staircase.

"Okay, if you guys say so . . ." Regina shrugged. "It was you who was afraid of becoming a colorful orb a second ago, Jasper, you suddenly got very brave."

"Someone this educated cannot possibly be dangerous," explained Jasper. "When I thought of the once-human, I thought of an uncivilized brute, not a scholar."

"So a scholar cannot possibly be a bad person, is that what you're saying?" Regina raised her eyebrows, but Jasper didn't answer. He was already going up the stairs. "Okay, I'll quote you on that later."

Regina, Joey and Brunorth followed Jasper up the dark staircase. When they stepped out on the other side of the hole, they found themselves in one of the two towers. The tower was long, dark and narrow, and it contained nothing except another staircase—a spiral one. The plant's light sneaked through the hole, but there was no other source of light in the tower. Where the stairs led to was not visible from the darkness.

Regina looked up at the long staircase, which faded into nothingness, and in that moment she wasn't afraid for some reason—she was determined.

"We're not stopping now, are we?" she said, smiling at the boys.

"Of course not." Joey smiled back.

Regina saw the same determination in Jasper's and Joey's eyes that she felt inside. This was why they were brought here.

They stepped on the iron staircase and made their way towards the top. The sound of the iron against the soles of their shoes echoed in the tall tower with each step. Their eyes grew accustomed to the dark by the time they reached the top of the staircase, so they could make out that there was a drop door on the ceiling, and the stairs led straight into it. Jasper opened the door, and as they stepped out on the other side, Regina's stomach clenched.

The walls in this room were not shiny, they appeared to be rotting as the dark paint was peeling off of them, revealing the revolting mold between the bricks. The room was filled with burning candles, and the walls were plastered with what looked like newspaper clippings. This space felt like the room of a madman.

"It's rotting from the inside," said Regina when she saw the exposed bricks.

"I'm more worried about these newspaper clippings," said Jasper.

"They're all about violent crimes," Joey said, examining the clippings.

Regina was the only one who didn't move. She stood at the edge of the drop door and kept looking at the different newspaper clippings with narrowed eyes, fearing what she might see. Some of them were recent, and others were extremely old, dating back to as early as 1620. The clippings didn't seem to have much in common; they were from different times, about different people, but two things were obviously clear: all of the articles were about some sort of violent act, and all of them had something handwritten next to them, usually just one word like *anger*, *greed* or *ill*.

"I have a word for whoever lives here: obsessive," said Joey.

"This one's about the Battle of Lützen!" said Jasper with excitement. "It's from 1632, wow! Any museum would give an arm and a leg for something like this."

"Why do people do such things?" asked Regina in a dying voice as she caught a glimpse of a particularly gruesome article—she didn't find all of this fascinating at all.

"The answer appears to be written on them," said Jasper, pointing at the handwritten words on the clippings. "It seems that the owner of this castle is looking for the answer to that question too."

"So the answers to humanity's problems are all here? Written on these clippings?" asked Regina with a healthy amount of skepticism.

"It's an interesting approach," said Jasper. "Whoever stuck these here spent a lot of time examining these events and the behavioral patterns behind them."

"Well, whoever lives here can't be that bad if he's interested in this stuff, right? He's not committing them, he's just trying to find answers. That's totally fine, right?" Regina asked, trying to convince herself mostly.

"These events cannot be explained with one word," said Joey quietly, his voice barely audible. "These things are so much more complex than they seem. You cannot explain the life and actions of a person with one word."

The boy's flow of spirits seemed to have disappeared as he was looking at one of the walls. His face looked pale in the candlelight. His sudden seriousness surprised Regina and Jasper.

"You're right," said Jasper, stepping away from the wall. "Some questions don't have definite answers."

Regina felt her heart beat faster and her stomach clutch as she was looking around the room, so she took a deep breath and closed her eyes for a moment. She refused to freak out again, how she had acted in front of the castle was embarrassing enough. The drop door they had come in through appeared to be the only exit, since the room had no other doors or windows, and this fact eased Regina's mind a little, since it meant that they would be turning back from here soon.

"I'm ready to leave if you guys are," she said when she

felt her anxiety overpower her patience.

"Brunorth is enjoying himself," said Jasper, looking at the tiny dragon, who was making friends with the flames of the candles.

Regina smiled as she looked at the tiny dragon, who didn't care about the big questions of life, he was simply playing with the flames, not aware of the articles on the walls around him. Regina didn't even notice that her anxiety had disappeared as she was admiring the carefree dragon, but the peaceful moment was interrupted by the loud sound of paper ripping.

Regina and Jasper turned around, and they saw Joey peeking out through a tiny hole on the wall.

"What happened?" Regina asked.

"I'm not sure," Joey answered with hesitation. "There's a bridge here."

Regina and Jasper rushed to Joey and looked out through the tiny hole. They saw a long, flimsy suspension bridge, which connected the tower they were in to the castle's other tower.

"This is a larger hole," said Joey as he examined the wall next to the tiny hole. "These newspapers are covering it."

"If we tear it down, we can cross the bridge," said Jasper.

"Should we tear it down?" Regina asked, hoping that they would still decide to turn back.

The wind answered her question when it pulled out all the newspaper clippings that were taped together in front of the large hole and carried them away.

"Well, at least we didn't have to tear it down ourselves," said Jasper with a shrug.

The bridge led to another hole on the other tower's top.

"I didn't see any other doors or windows, so I think this is the only way to the other tower," said Joey.

Jasper and Joey looked at each other and nodded, then they turned towards Regina, waiting for her approval on crossing the bridge. Regina hesitated a bit but nodded, hiding her reluctance as much as she could.

The hole on the wall was large enough for all of them to fit through easily. The cold wind gently rocked the bridge as they slowly made their way across it. The sun had set while they were in the castle, so it was hard to see where they were stepping in the night's gloom.

"Don't look down," said Jasper, who was the last one in line, after Joey, Regina and Brunorth.

As Jasper said that sentence, Regina instinctually looked down from the bridge. They were much higher up than she had thought they were. The castle's height must have been equivalent to a ten-story building's.

"Why did you say that? I didn't even think of looking down before you said that," said Regina, who was now grabbing onto the railing like her life depended on it.

"It's fine, just come on, don't stop," said Joey, turning around from the front. "Hold my hand," he added and reached back towards Regina.

Regina reached out for his hand, and with her other hand, she reached back towards Jasper.

"You should hold onto the railing," said Jasper.

"I'd rather hold onto you guys," said Regina with a smile.

Jasper smiled back, and he reached out to hold Regina's hand. They crossed the rest of the bridge holding hands, while Brunorth confidently waddled through next to them. After they stepped through the hole into the tower, they let go of each other's hands. Regina smiled to herself. She was grateful for the two boys' friendship.

They looked around the room, which was in a better condition than the previous one. The walls were crimson-colored, and the space was lit by shining plants, but not the same climbing plant as before. These plants were individual flowers placed on little shelves on the wall, and their petals were shining. A blood-red curtain divided the room in two, hiding the other side from the trio.

"Is that an apple?" asked Regina when she noticed the only thing in the room: a little table in front of the curtain with a bell jar on top, which was covering a golden apple.

They stepped closer to the table and took a closer look at the shiny gold apple. As they examined the fruit, they saw that a word was written on it.

"Kallistei," Regina read aloud.

"For the fairest one," Jasper translated.

"Indeed." An unfamiliar voice joined the conversation from the other side of the curtain, which now started to move upwards, exposing the rest of the room.

The trio stepped back, awaiting the reveal, but as the curtain disappeared into the ceiling, they only saw the back of a large and carefully crafted chair. The chair stood in front of differently sized and shaped glass balls, which were floating in the air. They appeared to be showing different scenes, and whoever was sitting in the chair must have been examining these scenes. He looked like an evil security guard, who was keeping his eyes on the world's events.

"I have been eagerly waiting for your arrival," said the man in the chair, whose voice sounded like he could burst out laughing any moment.

He slowly began turning his chair towards the trio. When it turned around, and they saw who was sitting in it, Regina involuntarily squeaked.

"I am Eris, enemy of the human race," the creature introduced himself.

6: THE ENEMY OF THE HUMAN RACE

There was no doubt that the creature sitting in the chair was the once-human in black. He looked like something that should have ceased existing a long time ago.

He was tall, bony, and the lump on his back was visible even with him sitting. The skin on the left side of his pale face looked cracked, and his eyes were different-colored. His right eye was brown, and his left eye was almost neon green, but not in a beautiful way; the neon green color on the cracked side of his face looked like it was caused by some sort of disease. His blond hair was like an old mop—long and dirty.

His body from the neck down looked like it was covered in a black scuba suit, but it was impossible to tell if the black layer was his clothing or his actual skin. His fingers underneath the black coating were unusually long, boney and sharp, and so were his feet.

As he looked the trio up and down, a large grin on his face made his appearance even more grotesque. He put the long, sharp fingers on his hands together as he examined the trio with a crazed expression.

"Regina White, Jasper Thorn and Joey Herd," he said with his filmy eyes wide open, which sparkled with manic excitement. "Such interesting specimens you are." His voice sounded like he was holding back laughter.

The way he looked at them would have made anybody forget their bravery. He seemed like he was about to swallow them whole. Neither of them dared to say a word. They just stared at the strange creature like defenseless rodents waiting for the predator's first move. Even Brunorth backed into the shade of one of the corners.

Eris slowly stood up and stepped in front of them. Standing up, it was even more outstanding how tall and strangely bony he was. He looked like his limbs and torso were stretched out, and his rubbery movements added to his weirdness. He bent down in front of Jasper and closely stared in his face with his mad, wide open eyes.

"Curiously intelligent, smart Jasper. Did you recognize this apple?" he asked as he awkwardly pointed at the bell jar with his long and black finger.

"It's the Apple of Discord," stuttered Jasper as he tried to avoid any eye contact with Eris.

"Exactly, exactly," Eris excitedly whispered in Jasper's face. "Interesting, isn't it? How a simple apple holds the power to start wars among humans? You just have to know where to throw it. What would I need to throw in front of you to get you to finally step over that line you've been walking on for so long now, hmm? You are so easily

controllable, Jasper, just one little push and—" He put both
of his hands over his mouth as he madly stared at Jasper,
who was looking at the floor in fear.

"Boom!" shouted Eris and burst out laughing for a brief
moment, but he turned back to being serious and quiet
immediately, almost like he wasn't allowed to laugh. "I will
use you in my research, and I just know that you will be a
wonderful specimen. I'll help you run over that line with a
passion! You'll see."

He looked Jasper up and down and licked his razor-thin,
pale lips, like he was getting ready to eat him up, but then he
abruptly turned his head towards Regina. His movements
were so awkward, it seemed like he didn't have any joints at

all.

"Kind-hearted, curious Regina. What a pretty girl you are," he said as he airily stepped in front of Regina. "We are a lot alike, you and I."

Eris softly touched Regina's face with his pointy fingers. Regina didn't back away, she looked Eris in the eye. The strange creature dispelled all of her fear somehow. It was like seeing a part of her own self for the very first time—he was too familiar to fear. Regina knew the emotion driving Eris all too well. She didn't find him neither interesting nor scary—she pitied him.

"It's an interesting thing, human behavior, isn't it? I know you're almost as interested in it as I am. I bet we could achieve great things together."

I don't want to be like you.

"What determination you have in your eyes, I'm surprised," said Eris as he let go of Regina's cheek with disappointment. "I thought you would be easier, you seemed so weak. I'm not giving up on you, I will be there when you have one of your weak moments and . . ." He clenched his fist like he had caught something in the air. The grin on his face got even larger as he stared at Regina with sinister eyes. Regina looked him straight in the eye. She was the most surprised by the fact that she wasn't frightened by Eris at all.

Eris slowly turned his head towards the last in line: Joey.

"Joey," he said, shaking his head with excitement. "We know each other well, don't we? I believe you have something of mine, don't you? I know you want to hide it from your new friends, but you can't hide who you are forever."

Joey looked unusually tense. Regina was surprised to see him so uneasy.

Eris quickly stepped in front of him and pulled out a newspaper clipping from Joey's pocket, the movement as quick as lightning.

"No, please," Joey pleaded as he tried to reach after the piece of paper in vain.

"Now, now, Joey. You shouldn't hide who you are from your friends. After all, you're a dangerous person, aren't you?" Eris pointed at the clipping.

"No . . . I'm not . . ." Joey tried to defend himself, but it seemed he didn't believe in his own innocence enough to form the words.

"But of course you are!" exclaimed Eris. "Don't be so sad, people like you make everything interesting!"

Eris raised the clipping in front of his own eyes and started reading it aloud with his almost caricature-like voice: "Boy's violent outburst sends father to hospital in critical condition."

"Shut up!" Joey shouted.

Regina's mouth opened from the surprise. She looked at Joey, who was staring at the ground in front of him. He looked helplessly angry as he clenched his fists and bit into his lips. Was Regina wrong about him? In that moment, it certainly seemed like it—Joey didn't have anything to say in his own defense.

"But why? Joey, why? Why did you do it?" Eris inquired as he stepped in front of Joey and lowered his head to face him closely. "The article doesn't say why you did it. Tell me why you did it, I need to know. What should I write on this piece of paper, huh? What should be your word?"

Regina looked at Jasper, who was just as stunned as she was. Joey still didn't say anything, he kept looking down, avoiding everybody's eyes. Regina noticed that his jaw was clenched as well; the little muscle on the side of his face kept popping in and out. Was he angry because he had been found out? That thought didn't sit right with Regina. The kind boy she had gotten to know couldn't have been such a monster.

"Tell me, Joey," Eris continued. "Tell me what turned you into such a freak!"

Regina saw a teardrop roll down Joey's face.

"Stop it!" she shouted for reasons she didn't quite understand herself.

Eris straightened up and looked at her in surprise.

"Regina," he said, almost disappointed. "You of all people should be just as curious as I am. You should know what lies inside of him, it's very important."

"No, it's not important," said Regina. "I don't care what's written on that stupid piece of paper. We don't know . . . Just leave him alone! Can't you see he's suffering? Don't you care?"

Eris listened to Regina intently. He looked more and more confused with every word she said, and after Regina finished, he looked at her with narrowed eyes for a short while, interpreting the information he had received. When he was ready to speak, his voice was quiet, and his expression showed that he was still deep in thought.

"Care, you ask? Do I care?" he thought out loud as he put his long arms behind his back and started pacing around the room. "I remember caring. The memory is very faint, but I remember having a heart that cared deeply. Deeply indeed."

Eris' voice had changed. He didn't sound like he was going to burst out laughing anymore. A hint of sadness sparkled in his mismatched eyes as he looked at Regina.

"Are you okay?" Regina asked, feeling pity for the miserable-looking creature again.

"Of course I'm okay, stupid girl," Eris answered, the madness slowly returning to his eyes, and his mouth forming a crazed grin again. "I've already made my choice a long time ago. The heart can't beat next to a mind full of questions." He pointed at his chest. "There's nothing inside here," he said. "It's all here." He raised his index finger to his temple. "It's what makes me strong."

Regina couldn't stop her face from slightly grimacing.

"You think you know anything better than me, little girl?" he asked, stepping in front of Regina. "I've spent multiple lifetimes acquiring the knowledge I have today, what do you know?"

Regina didn't answer, she just shrugged and shook her head. The last thing she wanted to do was make this strange creature mad.

"I'll tell you what you know. You know nothing. And you will never be as great as I am, because you're a fool. And you think you can teach me something? You? Teach me? Me?" His expression kept turning madder and madder.

"I am all-seeing! I am all-knowing! I am a self-made God!" he shouted as he turned his back to Regina and made his way to the other side of the room, where the glass balls were floating. "I can see everyone and everything through my precious spheres, nothing can be hidden from me," he continued quietly as he stood in front of the floating glass balls with his hands behind his back. "I will be watching you Regina White, Jasper Thorn and Joey Herd. I will be watching you, and when the time comes, you will see the power that I hold; this I promise you. Now get out of my castle."

He raised his right hand and snapped his fingers. As the sound pierced the air, the floor started to move beneath the trio. The dark floor flipped under them, and they all fell from the room.

A wide, spiral slide immediately caught them and guided them through the candle-lit tower. They were sliding down the slippery surface fast, so they didn't have time to panic or check where the slide was leading them, which was fortunate, because it was leading them to the very base of the castle, right into one of the walls, which opened right before they reached it, allowing them to fly out of the castle. The opening they flew out through was so close to the ground that they didn't get hurt as they landed on each other with Brunorth on top.

"Is everybody all right?" asked a familiar voice.

The bottom of a long brown robe was gliding through the grass in front of Regina. She immediately knew it was Agnitio.

"We're fine," replied the trio as Agnitio helped them up.

"Eris is quite the character, isn't he?" asked Agnitio with a smile.

"How can you let someone like that live here?" Jasper blurted out.

"Someone like that?" Agnitio looked confused. "Like what?"

"He's a foul creature, he's evil!" said Jasper.

"Oh, evil." Agnitio nodded and now seemed to understand what Jasper had meant. "There is no such thing as evil here."

"But he's spying on everyone!" Jasper was starting to lose his patience.

"Yes, I know, Jasper." Agnitio calmly placed his hand on Jasper's shoulder. "Evil is non-existent here as long as you don't choose to follow it yourself."

Even though he was as tall as Eris, he wasn't threatening at all—he exuded warmth and peace.

"Can he really control people?" Fear tainted Jasper's voice.

"No, Jasper, he can't. He might try his best to provoke you, but the choice of action remains yours. You have no reason to fear him, he can't make you do anything you don't want to do."

Jasper looked at him in silence as he processed what Agnitio had told him then nodded, showing that he understood what he had said. Agnitio smiled at him then straightened up and looked at Regina and Joey.

"How are you two?" he asked.

"Fine," replied Joey, wiping his eyes.

"Joey," said Agnitio, stepping in front of the boy, "don't let it break you. Let it build you up."

Joey raised his head and looked at the kind faun. His eyes became teary again as he thankfully nodded. Agnitio patted him on the shoulder.

"Agnitio?" said Regina quietly.

"Yes, Regina?"

"Eris, is he really human?"

"Yes. Eris is a human. Or 'was a human' is probably more accurate. He is thousands of years old. He came to Andara a long time ago, just like you three, he just refused to leave. He has been here ever since. He was always very interested in others. If he'd spent a little more time being interested in himself, maybe he wouldn't have become who you saw today. He has lost almost all of his humanity by now." Agnitio sadly shook his head as he looked up at Eris' tower.

"So, anyone can stay here forever?" asked Regina.

"We, Andarians, can't interfere with free will. Eris didn't want to go back, and now he can't, even if he wanted to, since so much time has passed. People come here from slightly different times, but they can't stay here and then go back to where they came from a hundred years later. That's against nature's law. Most people go back before the one month mark though. Someone staying here is extremely rare, since what brings one to Andara is the overpowering will to live, and staying here means giving up life."

"What was Eris like when he came here?" asked Regina.

"He was a charming young boy," remembered Agnitio. "He was so interested in everything in Andara. He made friends with a girl here. I remember them exploring this forest together. He grew quite fond of her. He wanted to stay here with her forever, never growing old, but her desires were different. She wished for a normal human life. Neither of them could persuade the other, so they parted ways. He isolated himself from then on. He started to show more interest in the people coming here than anything else. He hid in this forest and spied on the others from the shelter of the trees. He never had any other friends neither here nor back home, and he came from an orphanage, so he wasn't exactly homesick. He made it clear that he doesn't want to go back. Staying here means throwing away your life. Most creatures in Andara try to persuade the people who don't want to go back to return, but there are times when we are not successful. Human choice is an extremely strong force, we can't interfere with it."

Regina felt bad for the strange creature in the tower, who was once human, just like them. The realization that they could still become anyone towered over her as she looked up at the castle. After seeing Eris, she knew what she definitely wanted to avoid becoming.

"Are there others like him? Who chose to stay here?" she asked.

"Yes, the Living Dead. They live on the dark side of Dara Forest, they never make contact with visitors, and the visitors are not allowed in their part of the forest either. Eris is the only one who makes contact with the visitors. He is still interested in others, and I think he is a good person to learn from. A great anti-example if you will. Being faced with someone like him can be a strong force in building up who you don't want to become."

Regina felt safe in the tall faun's presence. Every muscle in her body eased up as she listened to him, and there were no traces left of the anxiety she had felt not so long ago.

"Why does he call himself the enemy of the human race?" asked Jasper.

"I believe it's a name the Trojans gave him after he wreaked some havoc among them. Eris created several situations that caused others to harm each other. He's especially proud of what he did with that apple. He wrote 'to the fairest one' on it and threw it in front of three sisters. The girls started to fight, because they all claimed that the apple was for them. Not knowing who threw the apple, they left Andara and went back home to ask their father which one of them was the most beautiful. The father refused to choose, so he asked a Trojan friend of his to answer the question for them. One of the girls promised him money if he chose her, the other precious jewels, and the third offered her own hand in marriage. The man chose the third girl, and he married her soon after, not knowing that the girl was already arranged to be wed to the king of Sparta. The Greeks saw this as great dishonor and soon attacked Troy. That's how Eris started the Trojan War with an apple. He was very proud of the nickname he had earned with that."

Agnitio looked concerned as he was telling the story. Regina felt uneasy seeing the wise faun looking up at the dark tower with a worried expression.

"I have another question," said Jasper. "I've been wondering about it a lot."

"Yes, Jasper?" Agnitio looked at Jasper, and the kind and calm expression returned to his face.

"Why is Andara called the Forbidden Land?"

"Ah, good question, Jasper, great question. You've seen it yourselves how many people choose to leave Andara right after they've arrived. People are often afraid of what they might see here. What you see can never be unseen, and that scares many. They'd rather cover their eyes and forbid themselves to stay here. But the truth is that the fate of the other world, your world, is in the hands of those who choose to stay."

Agnitio crouched down and petted Brunorth, who was curled up on his robe.

"As you've seen by now, Andara holds very dark creatures. As you journey onward, you will be faced with darkness you've never seen before. This road will take you to Mount Napharata. The sun doesn't shine over there, so the climate is a little different. Mount Napharata will be the most challenging destination of your journey. There are darker beings in this world than creatures who used to be human. And one way or another, they demand to be seen."

He straightened up and looked at the trio with a rare, serious expression on his face.

"This is the part where I'm supposed to tell you that it will not be scary. Well, it will be. But fear is not evil, it's natural. And strength can only be found inside of fear. So chase it. Your decision to stay carries greater influence than you could ever imagine."

Regina was not sure what to make of this advice, she didn't fully grasp Agnitio's words, so she simply nodded and hoped that she would understand when she needed to.

"It's getting very late," said Agnitio. "Come on, I'll take you somewhere you can spend the night."

Agnitio turned around and walked into the forest. The trio and Brunorth followed him. The trees were filled with little orbs that were shining like tiny light bulbs. Their warm light lit up the whole forest.

"They are called Dragontears," explained Agnitio when he saw how fascinated they all were with the beautiful lights. "The same plant grows in your huts."

It didn't take long before he stopped and turned towards them with a smile.

"We're here, you can spend the night here."

Regina looked around, and she didn't understand what Agnitio was talking about, since all she saw were trees. When Agnitio saw their confusion, he quickly pointed at the tree next to him.

"I meant this tree right here. You will find a familiar face in there. Have a pleasant night."

The trio stepped closer to the tree, and as they walked around it, they discovered a little door on the other side of the tree trunk. Regina turned around to thank Agnitio, but he was no longer there.

"Where did he go?" she asked Joey and Jasper.

"I'm not sure," Jasper answered, looking around. "He probably went home. Let's knock."

Jasper knocked on the door, and soon after, a familiar face peeked out through the cute little door: it was Y'sis. She looked even more magical as the warm light of the dark forest shined on her.

"Oh, hello, Regina, Jasper and Joey," she said, opening the door. "So nice to see you again. Come on in."

Regina stepped inside, carefully avoiding Y'sis' long white hair, which was all over the floor around her, the branch still tangled in it from before. Y'sis greeted them with a sweet smile, the colorful orbs dancing around her. Regina was surprised to see that the inside of the tree trunk was not as narrow as it seemed from outside. A whole little home lay inside it.

"Joey, aren't you coming?" Regina asked, turning around to look at Joey, who was still standing outside—he looked like he didn't want to join them.

"I think I'll just go somewhere else," said Joey, a defeated expression overpowering his face.

He turned around and began walking away. Regina ran out the door, after him. When she reached Joey, she gently placed her hand on his shoulder. Joey stopped and stared at the ground in front of him.

"Please stay, Joey," she said softly.

"It's better if I go. I'm not someone nice people like you should hang out with."

Joey attempted to continue on his way, but Regina tightened her grip on his shoulder, not allowing him to move forward.

"That's not true," she said. "I want to be your friend. I want to get to know you more."

She paused for a moment and thought of the newspaper article Eris had read out loud.

"And you don't know someone until you've seen their darkness," she continued. "That's what my grandpa used to say."

Joey turned around and looked her in the eye. The warm lights sparkled in his teary eyes. As Regina looked at the kind and funny boy, who now looked broken, she wanted to take away his pain. She didn't exactly know why, but she felt he didn't deserve to feel that way. She believed in his innocence.

She stepped closer to him and hugged him. Joey didn't move. He stood motionless in her embrace for a short while, but then he lifted his arms and hugged her back. They stood there like that for a couple of minutes.

"Are you coming back?" Regina asked as she gently let go of him.

Joey silently nodded. Regina smiled, and Joey smiled back from behind a face that was still torn. They made their way back to Y'sis' little tree home together.

7 THE NAYAKA

When Regina woke up the next morning, everyone was already up, only Brunorth was curled up next to her. She smiled at the thought that Joey, Jasper and Y'sis let her sleep in.

As she sat up and stretched her arms, she felt refreshed. She looked around the tiny room, which she had been too tired to examine last night. It was Y'sis' bedroom. The walls were circular and wooden, since they were inside a tree, but Regina still didn't understand how the inside of a tree could be so huge.

Colorful flowers and plants were growing on the light wooden walls, the floor and even the ceiling.

Regina, Jasper and Joey had slept on the floor, next to Y'sis' bed. The wood of the tree was surprisingly soft, and the big flowers growing on the floor served as comfortable pillows.

Regina got up and looked out the little round window. The sun's rays were bright, and the tree's wood was warm against her bare feet.

She heard the others talking, so she opened the little door and saw Jasper, Joey and Y'sis sitting around a little table, on the floor. The table was loaded with food and drinks, and their delicious smell filled the warm little room's air.

"Good morning, Regina," said Y'sis in her soft voice, almost singing.

"Good morning," Regina greeted them as well.

"Come, have some breakfast," said Y'sis, inviting her to the table, which also had flowers all over it.

Regina and Brunorth walked to the table and sat down between Jasper and Y'sis.

"Did you all sleep well?" Regina asked.

Joey and Jasper nodded, since their mouths were stuffed with food. Y'sis contentedly smiled as she watched them eat.

"You are quite the deep sleeper," said Y'sis. "You must have wonderful dreams."

"I don't really remember them," replied Regina and reached for something that looked like bread.

"That's Bol," explained Y'sis as Regina examined the bread-like food. "You should put some Maroon Bell on that," she added and handed a bowl of red jelly to Regina.

Regina dipped the Bol into the Maroon Bell and put it in her mouth. She wasn't surprised that it tasted wonderful. The flavor resembled bread and raspberry jam, just much better and more satisfying. Regina shared her food with Brunorth, who seemed to like it as well.

Regina noticed Y'sis admiring the markings on her arms that Joey had drawn. They looked like tattoos in some kind of ancient language.

"Are those really permanent?" Regina asked.

"Yes," Y'sis answered. "I made them permanent myself to enhance their power. Joey has an amazing talent. I have been waiting for his arrival for hundreds of years now."

She said that like it was the most ordinary thing in the world, but Regina, Joey and Jasper all stopped chewing their breakfast and looked at her in surprise.

"I thought those were just . . . doodles?" Joey said, stuttering.

"Oh, no, they're definitely not just doodles," said Y'sis. "You are a rare human—you are a Nayaka. You are able to

105

bless or curse others by drawing these signs, which are in the ancient language of the Nayakas."

"I'm able to what?" Joey asked in shock.

"Yes." Y'sis nodded. "You're a Nayaka. You just have to listen to your own heart to learn to control it."

"Does this mean . . . ? I mean, could this have . . . ? Wow, I have so many questions," Joey said, mumbling.

"That's okay," said Y'sis with a smile. "It's surprising news to get."

Regina and Jasper were both sitting with their mouths slightly opened, and their heads just kept turning left and right between Joey and Y'sis as they listened to the conversation.

"Could I have been using these powers without knowing it?" Joey asked when he could gather his words.

"Yes, you could have," said Y'sis. "When you felt extreme anger, fear, joy or love, your inner Nayaka could have cursed or blessed a person. It's all about feelings with Nayakas. I think you know one particular event for sure when your inner Nayaka took over your actions."

"So it was this . . ." Joey whispered, still trying to process the information. "But . . . I mean . . . Are you sure? No, it can't be."

Y'sis closed her eyes and slowly nodded her head.

"But it *can* be," she said. "The truth will remain the truth whether you believe it or not, you know."

Joey stared at Y'sis in silence for a short while. Y'sis poured herself some tea and kept patiently sipping it as Joey processed what she had said. It seemed like Joey was arguing with himself on the inside and couldn't decide if he should believe what he had heard or not.

"How did you know that I will not hurt you?" he asked, breaking his silence.

"I feel the beating of your heart," said Y'sis, smiling at Joey. "You are not the monster you think you are."

"I can't believe it." Joey shook his head.

"You don't need to strive. It will come as you listen to the beating of your own heart."

Joey silently nodded, and his eyes travelled to the drawings on Y'sis' arms.

"What are those exactly?"

"They are different blessings in the ancient language of the Nayakas. You are one of their descendants. Most souls are colorful, like the ones around me, but your soul is white, the rarest of them all. You have the soul of a Nayaka."

"Wow," said Joey, mumbling again. "So," he continued, trying to gather his thoughts, "I'm a Nayaka. I can bless or curse people, and I can learn how to use this power by listening to the beating of my own heart."

"Exactly, yes." Y'sis nodded. "But there is something else. Being a Nayaka carries even greater responsibility than being an ordinary human. You see, Nayakas are the purest of humans, but being pure has its own weaknesses—a Nayaka's soul is easily corrupted. Think of them like cups of water. Even a tiny drop of paint can change their color. The paint being their own feelings in this case—they are easily ruled by them. And when a Nayaka is overpowered by a feeling—love, fear, anger or gratitude—they bring their powers forth, blessing or cursing a person. That's why it's so important for a Nayaka to learn to govern themselves by listening to the beating of their own heart. Because they are humans after all, they have free will. If they allow their heart to be overpowered by anger or hatred and make a decision that does harm to the greater good, their inner Nayaka will turn into a Danava, transforming their soul from white to black and haunting them for all eternity. It's very hard to recover a blackened soul. Very hard."

Joey's face turned ghostly white as he listened to Y'sis, who didn't seem to notice the effect her words had on Joey.

"But don't worry, Nayakas are inherently kind and loving creatures," she added when she looked at Joey. "But, like all humans, they can also lose their way. Just listen to the beating of your own heart, okay, dear Joey? Just smile, breathe and listen."

Y'sis smiled from ear to ear at Joey then took a sip from her floral teacup as she acknowledged that she had let Joey know his origins.

Regina and Jasper turned to Joey. They were both a little concerned, not knowing themselves how to process this information.

"Are you okay?" Regina asked.

"I think so," said Joey, still confused.

"This must have answer a lot of questions for you," said Jasper.

"It actually does." Joey nodded. "So many questions . . ."

"At least you have the answers now," said Regina, smiling. "And being a Nayaka sounds pretty awesome."

"Except for the eternal damnation part," Jasper added.

"I only know of one Nayaka who turned into a Danava," said Y'sis. "Even though countless Nayakas have been born since the beginning of time, only one of them lost this personal battle you Nayakas face. This person actually changed the course of humanity. Not in a good direction. Oh well, that's just how it is." Y'sis easily dismissed her own train of thought and continued sipping her tea.

Regina smiled as she looked at the confused Joey. She was glad that she listened to her instincts about him. Joey always seemed like a kind-hearted person to her, and now she knew for sure that he almost definitely was one. She couldn't imagine him ever turning into a Danava.

"Don't think too much about it," Y'sis advised Joey as she poured all three of them some tea.

"Thank you, Y'sis. Thank you for telling me."

"You're welcome," said Y'sis with a big smile. "It's one of my duties to welcome the Nayakas. I quite like your kind. I should be thanking you for the blessing. It helps me a lot with my job as a Guardian, so thank you, Joey."

"You're welcome." Joey scratched his head and let out an embarrassed little laugh.

"Drink your tea, everyone." Y'sis stood up from the table. "You should be on your way soon."

The trio reached for their teacups and drank the liquid

inside. Once they finished their drinks and acknowledged that it was delicious and surprisingly energizing, they got up from the table and thanked Y'sis for the breakfast and for allowing them to stay in her little tree home for the night.

"It was my pleasure," said Y'sis with a smile as she saw them to the door. "You're going to Mount Napharata now, right? Just go straight ahead, you can't miss it. The Red Queen is quite the unpleasant woman, but I'm sure you can handle her. When in doubt, look at the stars."

The trio and Brunorth walked out the door, and they set off through the forest. Y'sis stood in the door and waved goodbye to them until they disappeared among the trees. Regina smiled as she looked back at Y'sis. Her long white hair, which covered the ground around her, the antlers on her head and the colorful orbs dancing next to her made her the cutest creature Regina had ever met, and that included all the fictional characters she had read about. She didn't even think about where they were going as she waved back to the short creature.

"How are you doing? Did you manage to process all that new information?" Jasper asked Joey.

"I don't think it's possible to process it," said Joey. "But at least I know now what's happening to me. There were a few times when it took over me, and it was really scary."

"Like with your father?" asked Jasper.

"Jasper!" Regina yelled at Jasper in warning.

"It's okay, Regina." Joey didn't seem to mind the question and remained calm. "Yes, like with my father."

110

"You don't have to talk about it." Regina wanted to make sure Joey was not going to talk about something he was not ready to talk about.

"It's okay, you're my friends," Joey said with a smile. "Long story short: my father is a drunk, and he tried to hurt my mother one night. I defended her and don't really remember what happened after that. All I know is that my father ended up at the bottom of the stairs. He got really hurt, and when he was asked what had happened to him, he told everyone I attacked him out of the blue. His story even got into the news somehow."

"Wow, that's crazy, I'm so sorry," said Regina.

"Is your mom okay?" asked Jasper.

"Yes, she's fine. My dad's still in the hospital though. I told my mom that we should leave while he's in there, but she doesn't want to leave him. I tried to persuade her to go, I even packed our suitcases, but I just ended up on the street by myself. I don't understand her."

"Only she can make her own choices," said Jasper consolingly.

"I know, but it's just so hard to accept it. Thank you for not judging me. It feels good to finally talk about it to someone. I still feel horrible about all of it. I know I'm a Nayaka and all that, but still. I wish things would have happened . . . differently."

"It's not your fault," said Regina. "You did the right thing."

Joey didn't answer. It was obvious that he still didn't let

111

go of the blame he had placed on himself.

Regina was glad that he was at least confident enough to talk about what had happened with his family. He was still confused, but the teary-eyed boy who looked so broken and torn seemed far away in that moment.

"Hey, Jasmine!" shouted a deep, unnerving voice from among the trees.

"Oh, please, no." Jasper sighed, because he identified the voice immediately.

"How you doing, earthworm?" Clive appeared between the trees, followed by Pyro and Snow.

"You didn't wet yourself yet and run home? I'm surprised." Clive laughed and put his elbow on Jasper's shoulder.

Brunorth quietly growled at the large boy.

"Leave him alone!" Regina pulled Jasper closer to herself and farther away from Clive.

Jasper just stood defeated and looked at the ground in front of him, accepting the situation.

"Don't interrupt, little girl, the big men are talking. Or at least one big man is talking, right Jasmine?" Clive pulled Jasper back next to himself.

"Hey, dude, leave him alone, okay?" Joey stepped next to Jasper.

"Wow, I don't even know this guy." Clive turned towards Pyro, who was standing a few feet away from them, watching the events with a smug smile on his face. "Would you mind your own business, stranger?"

"No, I will not." Joey's voice was firm.

"Pyro, what do you think about this new jerk?"

"I think he should shut his pie hole and mind his own business," Pyro replied as he walked next to Clive.

"Pyro, don't," Snow whispered, trying to grab Pyro's arm, but the boy aggressively pulled it out of her hands and proceeded forward.

"So you got yourself a bodyguard? The little girl is not enough anymore to protect you?"

Clive laughed at Pyro's remark like a pig choking on its food. He looked like his jaw was going to fall out, he opened his mouth so wide.

"You should maybe build a robot, because these wimps won't be enough to save you, Jasmine," Clive added as he wiped the drool off his chin.

"Can't you just leave me alone?" asked Jasper. "At least here?"

"Umm, let me think about it. No!" Clive laughed like a pig again.

Every muscle in Regina's body tensed up as she watched the events. She felt helpless. She looked at Snow, who was still standing farther away from the scene. She seemed uncomfortable and uneasy. Pyro and Clive towered over the short Jasper, and Joey was protectively standing next to him.

"Let's just go." Joey tried to pull Jasper away from the two boys.

"Don't even think about it, hero!" yelled Clive and pushed Joey, who fell on the ground.

"Just, please, stop it!" Regina shouted.

"Shut your face already!" Clive grabbed Jasper's collar.

Regina looked at Joey, who had his eyed closed. *What is he doing? Is he hurt too?* Regina had had enough. She walked up to Clive and began trying to peel his fingers off Jasper's collar. Her attempt to free Jasper was not successful. Clive's giant hand was impossible to move, and the enormous boy only laughed at her effort.

"Here, big guy, take this." Joey had arrived next to them and was handing Clive a leaf he had probably found on the ground. "Consider it a peaceful gift."

"Are you serious?" Clive's voice was crackling with suppressed laughter. "What are you? Some kind of nature boy? A fairy maybe? This is hilarious."

Clive took the leaf from Joey, and Regina noticed that something was carved into it—a strange sign. Clive burst out laughing, but his fun didn't last long. He suddenly started gasping for air, and he let go of Jasper as he reached for his own throat in despair.

"What the heck did you do, man?" Pyro asked as he helplessly stood next to his choking friend.

"Come on, let's go," whispered Joey and grabbed Regina and Jasper. "He'll be fine. I hope."

Regina looked back as they fled the scene, and she saw Snow and Pyro supporting Clive from the sides. Snow caught Regina's eyes, and looked at her questioningly. Regina didn't really know what message to send Snow, so she just returned her look with a half-smile, trying to signal

114

that Clive would probably be okay.

"Thanks Joey," said Jasper, gasping.

"You're welcome. I'm sorry it took so long. I don't really know what I'm doing."

"What did you do? Did you curse him?" Regina asked.

"I think so. I did what Y'sis told me, I listened to the beating go my heart and the rest just sort of happened. I have no idea what just happened to be honest."

"It was really cool," said Jasper, smiling. "I don't even know what would have happened if you weren't there. So helping me was in the benefit of the greater good, huh?"

"I really hope so," said Joey, still running. "I don't see how shutting down that guy would not benefit the greater good though. Do they go to the same school as you guys?"

"Yeah. Pyro and his sidekick, Clive. I've had the pleasure of attending the same school as them since the fourth grade. They've been at me since the very first day Pyro transferred to our school. I've gotten used to it by now."

"You shouldn't get used to stuff like that, that's just wrong," said Joey.

Regina and Brunorth dropped behind the two boys as they all gradually slowed down. She listened to their conversation, trying to process what had happened. Confrontations like this took a lot out of her, especially when she was unable to help. She didn't understand why Clive and Pyro acted the way they did, but after meeting Eris, she didn't even want to think about it anymore. *It is what it is.*

She raised her head up towards the sky. She could see little pieces of the clear sky between the bushy green trees. Regina lost all her troubling thoughts as she looked at the millions of stars sparkling on the light blue sky.

She smiled and a thought came to her mind: *When in doubt, look at the stars.* Y'sis' words jingled in her mind, and in that moment, Regina understood what they meant. Looking at the stars in the sky, all her troubles seemed unimportant, and life felt airy altogether.

Regina felt so at ease in that moment that she closed her eyes, letting the sun's rays shine on her face. She got so submerged in the moment that she didn't realize the boys had stopped, so she bumped into Joey's back.

"What are you doing?" asked Joey, laughing. "Are you okay?"

"I'm fine, sorry." Regina rubbed her nose. "Why did we stop?"

"That's why." Jasper pointed at something in front of them.

Regina stepped out from behind Joey, and her mouth fell open when she saw what lay ahead. The sun didn't shine on the road before them. The forest ended, and the richly green grass and trees turned into a sandy, empty and dark desert.

"But . . . how?" Regina turned her head towards the sky again to check if the sun was still shining—it was shining brightly on the forest, but its rays didn't reach the dark desert.

"Something might be blocking the sun," said Jasper, who

also looked baffled.

"Agnitio did mention that the sun doesn't shine here, but this is somehow not how I imagined it," said Joey.

They looked at the dark, seemingly endless desert in front of them as Brunorth sneaked up to the sharp line that divided the green, lively grass and the dark, lifeless sand, and he sniffed it.

"Are we ready for the most challenging destination of our journey?" asked Joey with a smile on his face.

Regina and Jasper nodded.

"What do you guys think we'll find there?" asked Regina.

"I have no idea," said Joey.

"I have a feeling it's not something pleasant," said Jasper, still staring at the darkness in front of them.

They took a last deep breath of the forest's clean air and stepped over the line between light and dark together, headed towards the unknown darkness of the endless desert.

8: MOUNT NAPHARATA

The sky was pitch black above them. The stars, which were visible from other parts of Andara, even during daytime, were nowhere to be seen. The warm air was foggy and quiet. Only the sound of their steps could be heard in the red sand.

The trio and Brunorth continued on their way through the foggy desert in silence, until they heard the sound of waves crashing.

"Is that . . . water?" asked Joey as they stopped to listen to the sound.

"Sounds like it," said Regina.

"In the middle of the desert?" Jasper raised his eyebrows.

"Maybe it's a mirage," said Regina. "Wait, do mirages have sound?"

"No, they don't," said Jasper. "Mirages are optical phenomena."

"So, there must be water nearby," concluded Joey. "Let's watch our step then."

They proceeded with cautious steps as the sound of the waves got louder and louder. Soon they reached the source

118

of the sound. The wide desert turned into a narrow path in front of them, dark waves of the sea violently crashing into both sides.

The trio stopped before the path. Brunorth stepped towards the water and cautiously sniffed it. He didn't seem to sympathize with it as he crawled backwards with an unfriendly growl.

"I feel you, little friend," said Regina. "I don't like this either."

"Well, we can't say we weren't warned," said Joey. "Agnitio was pretty clear about this place."

"Do you hear that?" Jasper asked them.

"What?" Regina tried to listen for a sound. "I can't hear anything."

"Listen," said Jasper, whispering.

Regina, Jasper and Joey quietly stood staring at the foggy darkness above the violent sea, and they listened to the sound of the land. Somewhere beyond the noise of the mad waves, Regina could make out a faint sound: a woman screaming.

"Is that . . . a scream?" asked Joey.

"Sounds like it," said Jasper.

Regina gathered her brows. What was going on on the other end of this path? Was someone being tortured? What would happen to them on their arrival? Should they just turn back? Or should they try to help whoever was screaming?

She looked at Joey and Jasper, who were trying to hear the scream among the noise of the sea. They looked just as worried as Regina felt.

"What should we do?" she asked.

"We're going, there's no doubt about that, right?" said Joey, unsure about his words. "I mean, that's why we're here."

"If we don't go, the only other option is to go back home," said Jasper.

Regina turned her head towards the dark water again. The distance was swallowed by the fog. As Regina stared into the gloom, debating what to do, the uncertain darkness reminded her of the alley where she had met Agnitio. She didn't want to turn back.

"Are we ready to go then?" she asked the boys with determination.

Jasper and Joey nodded.

"We should go behind each other," said Joey. "This road's pretty narrow."

"Good idea," said Regina and stepped on the narrow path, leading the way.

As soon as Brunorth saw that Regina had set off on the unfriendly path, he quickly stumbled next to her in a protective stance, growling at the water. Regina smiled and petted the head of her little but fierce friend. She looked back to check on the boys. Joey was behind him, and he was followed by Jasper.

Nothing happened for a while as they were walking on the sandy path. They took their steps cautiously, but as they kept on walking, the path seemed more and more endless.

The waves were crashing next to them, and Brunorth kept growling at the dark water. The scream could still be heard beneath the noise of the mad sea, but the source of it didn't seem to come closer with their steps.

They continued on the narrow path for a while, their steps becoming more and more confident with each minute. Just as Regina started to feel self-assured on her feet, the scream suddenly became much louder. It was not muffled by the sound of the waves anymore. The trio froze as the sharp scream rapidly approached them.

"Duck!" shouted Joey, jumping towards Regina and tackling her to the ground.

Regina landed on her back, the air pushed out of her lungs. As she lay on the ground, she saw the one screaming fly over her. She felt like time suddenly slowed down, and she was watching it fly over her in slow-motion.

The creature had long red hair, she was slim, and where her legs should have been, she had a fishtail—she was a mermaid.

As the mermaid flew over Regina, her mouth was wide open as she screamed. Her teeth were not like human teeth, they looked long and sharp, much like the teeth of a shark. Her scream was unbearable not muffled by the water. Regina felt every inch of her body ache as she endured the sound.

It felt like forever before the mermaid finally landed in the water on the other side of the path. The screaming stopped the moment she disappeared in the dark water.

Regina's body still shivered from the soul-shattering scream, and she felt Joey, who was on top of her, shaking too.

"Are you okay?" she asked with her ears still ringing.

"I'm fine," said Joey, staggering to his feet. "Are you?"

Regina nodded in reply.

Joey threaded his fingers into his raven-black hair to sweep it out of his face, and he reached towards Regina to help her up.

Regina's body was still in pain, her ears were ringing, but as she looked at Joey, whose hair was blowing in the wind, her chest felt warm inside.

"Thank you," she said, reaching for his hand and letting him help her up.

They both turned towards Jasper, who was standing like his legs had rooted into the ground.

"Are you okay?" Regina asked.

"Yes, I'm fine," said Jasper, still looking shocked. "What in the world was that?"

"It looked like some kind of evil mermaid," said Regina, rubbing her ears.

"It looked really mad at you," said Joey, who was also rubbing his ears.

"At me?" Regina asked, surprised.

"Yeah," said Jasper, agreeing with Joey. "I saw it too."

"Did I do something?" Regina asked, not understanding what she could have done to make the mermaid mad.

"I don't think so," said Jasper.

"Maybe she just didn't sympathize with you," said Joey with a shrug. "It happens."

"Great," said Regina and looked at Brunorth, who was growling at the water even more angrily than before.

Regina couldn't hear the scream anymore, but she was not sure if that was because it had stopped, or because her ringing ears just couldn't hear it anymore.

Brunorth continued to growl at the water.

"You can calm down now, she's gone," Regina said to the tiny dragon as she crouched down next to him.

She petted his head, and her eyes wandered to the spot in the water at which Brunorth was growling. Her heart almost fell out of her chest. A pair of eyes was looking at her from beneath the surface of the water. The mermaid didn't swim away—it was right there, staring at her.

Regina didn't dare move, so she stayed in the same position as she gently tried to pull the growling Brunorth farther away from the water.

"We should go," said Jasper. "That creature might come back, and I don't want to be here for that."

"Mmm . . ." whimpered Regina, still looking into the creature's eyes, too afraid to move.

"What's wrong?" asked Joey and stepped next to Regina.

The silence that followed revealed to Regina that Joey now saw the creature too.

The mermaid started to emerge from the water. As she slowly made herself visible, she was looking at Joey, and her mouth distorted into a strange smile. The abnormally large teeth in her mouth made her look grotesque.

"Hello, pretty boy," said the creature in a voice that sounded more like a chainsaw than human speech.

"Hi . . ." Joey stuttered.

"Boys like you are rare here," said the mermaid, her voice a pain to hear.

Her movements told that she tried to look charming, but she looked more bizarre than anything. Her long and sharp teeth even made her have a lisp.

"You have very bad taste," she continued. "Boys like you shouldn't lay eyes on girls like this." She said the last word with disgust, looking at Regina, who felt blood rush to her cheeks. "Boys like you don't belong here." She raised her eyes to Joey again, and she reached out towards his legs, pushing Regina aside in the process. "You belong somewhere so much better than this. You deserve so much better." She slowly started to crawl out of the water, never breaking eye-contact with Joey.

Regina looked at Joey, who seemed strangely stiff. He wasn't blinking and kept staring at the mermaid like he was under a spell.

"I will take you somewhere you belong," said the creature, crawling closer to Joey. "I will make you feel things you deserve, I will treat you like the king you are."

The mermaid crawled next to Joey, and she grabbed his leg. Joey was still staring at her with empty eyes.

"Joey," said Regina in a dying voice.

Joey broke eye-contact with the mermaid on the sound of

Regina's voice, and he seemed as if he was searching for the speaker.

The mermaid became infuriated by Joey's reaction. Her bizarre smile turned into a violent snarl, then she released her soul-shattering scream as she pulled on Joey's legs, who fell on his back. The mermaid tried to pull him into the water with her, but Regina and Jasper jumped towards them and grabbed Joey's arms. The mermaid continued screaming as she violently tried to pull Joey into the water.

"Let him go, you crazy!" Jasper shouted, clenching his teeth in strain.

Regina and Jasper both tried to pull Joey with all their strength, but the mermaid was very strong. Regina felt that she was stronger than her and Jasper together. Joey's eyes were still empty as he was staring into nothingness. His legs were already in the water, and Regina felt like she couldn't hold onto him much longer. Her eyes became teary as she gathered all her strength and grabbed onto Joey as hard as she could, but it still seemed like her and Jasper's strength would not be enough against the screaming mermaid. Joey became more and more submerged in the water. Regina's and Jasper's feet were on the edge of the narrow path when a large flame covered the mermaid. Regina and Jasper fell back with Joey in their arms as the mermaid screamed painfully then disappeared under the water.

"Brunorth," Regina said, gasping, with tears in her eyes.

The source of the large flame was the tiny dragon. He was now sitting, looking at them with a proud expression on his face.

"What happened?" asked Joey as he sat up and rubbed his arms.

"The mermaid tried to entice you and take you to her world," said Jasper, panting.

"Brunorth saved us," Regina added, touched. "He breathed fire for the first time! Right in her face!"

"It was pretty cool," said Jasper. "Way to go, Brunorth!"

"You saved us, little friend." Regina hugged the tiny dragon. "Thank you."

Regina kissed Brunorth's head and got up from the ground along with Joey and Jasper.

"Wow, okay," said Joey, trying to process what had just happened. "I really want this path to end now," he added as he tried to wring the water out of his jeans.

"Me too, but this makes me wonder what is waiting for us at the end of this path," said Regina. "This place is not very promising so far."

"Well, it's supposed to be the most challenging destination in Andara," said Jasper. "Basically anything could be waiting for us up ahead. Somehow I feel that it's going to be much worse than a screaming mermaid."

"You're right," agreed Joey. "We should be ready to face anything."

Regina didn't want to think about what was waiting for them at the end of the narrow path, wrapped in the fog. She knew that she wanted to continue on, so there was no use thinking about it. She watched Joey as he tried to eliminate as much water from his jeans as he could, then they proceeded on the narrow path.

It didn't take long before they finally reached the end. The narrow road turned into a wide desert once again, and water was nowhere to be seen anymore, only endless, dark sand.

They were relieved to step out from between the loud waves.

"At least there won't be any mermaids now," said Joey as they stood next to each other again.

"No, but there's something else." Jasper pointed at the dark sky.

Regina raised her head, and she saw something flying above them, but it was too dark to make out what it was exactly. She could only conclude that it was a black creature flying in circles above them in the black sky.

"What is that?" she asked.

"A crow maybe?" guessed Joey. "I'm not sure."

"It looks bigger than a crow," said Jasper.

"It's a pegasus," answered a familiar voice.

Regina froze up to the sound of the unnerving voice that was coming from the fog in front of them. She knew exactly who the voice belonged to.

"They are majestic creatures," the voice continued. "They were white once, but because they refused to fit in with the others, they turned black. They broke away from the herd and became solitary creatures. Awesome animals."

A figure slowly emerged from the veil of the fog—it was

Tom, Regina's brother.

"Hey, little sis," he said as he came closer to them with his hands in his pockets and a smug look on his face. "So you came to where the real stuff goes down. I have to admit that I didn't think you'll make it here."

"What are you doing here?" Regina asked with mild shock. "I didn't think this was your kind of place."

"But of course it is, little sis!" said Tom, raising his voice, making it even more unnerving than his usual tone. "This is where all the possibilities lie! I'm going to take advantage of everything here and make it big when I go home. How come you're still here, though?"

"I wanted to stay," Regina answered timidly—her brother's tone made her feel like she was not important enough to be in Andara. "I like Andara."

"Well, Mount Napharata might be too hardcore for you," said Tom, laughing. "It's no playground, like the other places here. The Red Queen doesn't take kindly to weaklings."

"Isn't she nice, like Agnitio?" Regina asked, without reacting to her brother's usual insult.

"Agnitio?" Tom asked, his voice filled with disdain. "Who the heck is Agnitio? The Red Queen was the one who brought me here, and she's the only one I'm interested in here. She can give me what I need."

Regina quietly nodded. She didn't even want to try telling his brother about Agnitio and the others, since she knew he wouldn't be interested anyway.

"Is that a dragon?" Tom asked and stepped closer to Brunorth.

"Oh, yeah," said Regina, wishing she could just leave the scene. "That's Brunorth."

Brunorth violently growled at Tom's approach. The tiny dragon lowered his head and suspiciously snarled behind his little dragon mustache.

"Brunorth," repeated Tom as he crouched in front of the dragon. "What a stupid name. Did you give it to him?"

"Yes . . ." said Regina with sadness in her voice.

Tom must have been too close to Brunorth, because the tiny dragon suddenly had enough of his presence and bit his knee.

"Oh." Tom smiled and stood up. He made it seem like the bite didn't hurt at all. Even his smile was somehow foul.

"I like the pegasus better," said Tom and turned around. "See you later, little sis."

The trio stood silently as Tom disappeared into the foggy darkness from where he had come. Brunorth only stopped growling when he was nowhere to be seen anymore.

"So that was your brother," said Joey in a sympathizing tone.

"Pleasant fellow, isn't he?" said Jasper.

Regina didn't say anything, she just rested her eyes on the upset Brunorth, who was looking at her as well, and let out a tired sigh.

"Let's just go," she said and proceeded forward, avoiding the direction her brother had taken.

Every time Regina made contact with her brother, he made her feel small and worthless. She was afraid that Jasper and Joey might see her the same way because of Tom's remarks. Jasper already knew Tom, but Regina still tried to avoid situations where her friends could make contact with her brother—she didn't want them to see how Tom saw her.

Jasper and Joey probably understood that she didn't want to talk about her brother, because they never mentioned him again.

"I'm really proud of little Brunorth," said Joey, trying to divert Regina's attention when he caught up to her.

"Me too," said Regina and smiled at Joey, thanking him for his attempt.

As they proceeded forward, something became visible in front of them as it emerged from the fog. A large mountain as black as the darkness towered over them.

"I think we reached Mount Napharata," said Jasper.

The large mountain was almost unnoticeable, it blended into the darkness so well.

As they stood in front of Mount Napharata, a violent roar tore into the air. They immediately turned their heads upwards. The sky above them was occupied by an enormous black dragon, who was charging towards them. The trio didn't even have time to react before the large dragon landed in front of them, surrounding itself in a huge cloud of dust. It let out another violent roar as it was menacingly standing before them. The creature was so large that its teeth alone were bigger than Regina.

All three of them stood frozen in front of the enormous creature, who could have easily swallowed all of them whole.

Amidst the warm roar of the large dragon, Regina didn't even notice that Brunorth had waddled away from her. He was happily jumping towards the large creature.

"Saphira?" whispered Regina when she saw the tiny dragon's reaction.

The large dragon stopped roaring when Brunorth reached

her. She gently rubbed her spiked black head against the tiny dragon, then she softly grabbed the little creature with her teeth, opened her enormous wings and lifted off into the sky.

"Brunorth, no!" Regina yelled as her little friend disappeared in the darkness of the sky. "No, please, don't take him away!" Pain echoed in her voice.

She tried to run after the large dragon, but Saphira quickly disappeared in the distance along with Brunorth.

Regina fell on her knees. Her eyes were filled with tears as she realized that Brunorth was gone. She felt two hands touch her shoulders.

"You will see him again, don't worry," said Joey.

"A friendship like that doesn't just end," said Jasper.

Regina was calmed a bit by the words of her friends. She agreed—Brunorth's and her friendship couldn't possibly have ended here. She reached for both Joey's and Jasper's hand, and they pulled her up from the red sand together. Regina thanked her friends' compassion with a smile.

"What a touching scene."

A woman's unfriendly voice tainted the loving atmosphere of the trio. They all turned to look at the speaker. Regina wiped the tears from her eyes, so she could see the owner of the deep voice.

A tall, curvy woman was standing in a doorway that opened from the mountain. The curls of her hair were long and blood-red. The red color almost vibrated in the dark. She was leaning at the doorway; her curves were especially prominent in that position. The long black silk dress that was flowing against her body left almost nothing to the imagination. Her unfriendly wrinkles were still visible under the pretty mask of heavy makeup on her face. A wicked smile stretched across her face as she looked at the trio.

"Welcome to Mount Napharata. I am Bellator, the Red Queen."

9: SWALLOWED BY DARKNESS

"Mama dragon took her baby back?" said the Red Queen with a hint of ridicule in her voice, still leaning on the doorway that opened from the black mountain. "How dare she, right? Take away your friend, who she abandoned for her own selfish reasons. You must feel very sad."

"I'm fine," said Regina, keeping her distance from the woman. "We'll meet again, I'm sure."

The Red Queen raised her eyebrows.

"You can't just believe that it will be how you want it to be," she said. "You have to take matters into your own hands. Others don't care about what you want. Everybody's looking out for themselves, even dragons. You have to take what you want, otherwise you will never have it."

Regina thought that what the Red Queen was saying made sense, but somehow she felt a strange dislike towards her. She pressed her lips together and silently nodded, but the Red Queen sensed her distance. She narrowed her eyes and angrily pushed herself away from the wall she was leaning on.

134

"You will never reach what you want with that attitude," she said, her voice like a hiss. "You could learn a thing or two from your friend over here."

She glided next to Jasper, and her dress moved on her body like it was made from some kind of dark liquid rather than silk.

"Now, *you* have potential," she said, leaning over and softly touching Jasper's chin.

She, too, was surprisingly tall. As she was leaning forward in front of Jasper, her large chest sprung up, right before Jasper's eyes. The boy's face became red like a tomato, and he tried to avert his eyes.

A satisfied smile stretched across the Red Queen's face as she saw Jasper's unease.

"You went through so much," she said in an appreciative tone as she straightened up. "Still, here you are, standing stronger than ever. You have so much potential, Jasper. Mount Napharata is exactly the place for you. We can help you reach your full potential. You can become someone who stands above others. With your intellect, it won't even be hard. Lord Ate will be happy to have someone like you."

"Well, thank you," said Jasper, a bit disoriented.

"You'll love it here." The Red Queen winked at Jasper.

She then turned towards Joey, but instead of speaking to him, she just looked at him intensely. Her eyes slowly widened as she analyzed Joey. Her expression became slightly terrified. She quickly averted her eyes from the boy and began speaking to Regina and Jasper, like Joey was not even there.

"So, there's something you don't know," she said, trying to gain back her composure. "You all came from the Field of Cetana. But that's not the only camp in Andara. Agnitio isn't the only one bringing people here—my job is the same. But as you might have guessed, the camp here is different— I choose my people wisely. I don't just present anyone to Lord Ate, only those who truly have potential."

Jasper began to open his mouth, probably trying to ask who Lord Ate was, but the Red Queen didn't let him speak.

"Lord Ate," she continued, raising her finger to silence Jasper, like she knew what he was about to ask, "is the one who we at Mount Napharata accepted as our leader. He is the most powerful being in existence, and he helps us all reach who we were destined to be. We believe that only with his guidance can we reach true happiness. If you choose to join us, what you will learn here will guide you towards happiness and success back home. You all were brought here by Agnitio, which means that you will have to work a little harder, but you are most welcome to join us. I see potential in all of you."

The wicked smile stretched across her face again, and she put her long red fingernails together in front of her large chest, awaiting the trio's reaction with content. Regina, Jasper and Joey, however, were all looking at her with confusion on their faces, not exactly impressed.

"So, you guys are against Agnitio and the others?" Regina asked.

"Well, I wouldn't say against," said the Red Queen, slightly rolling her eyes. "I would say . . . we view things differently." She seemed like she was starting to lose her patience. "If you don't see how huge of an honor it is to choose the camp here at Mount Napharata, then even Lord Ate can't save you!" She resentfully turned her back on them and set off towards the doorway she had come from.

Regina looked at Joey, who shrugged, indicating that he doesn't get the strange woman either, and that they're probably better off not getting mixed up with her.

"Wait!" yelled Jasper.

Regina and Joey questioningly looked at him, and Regina even poked him with her elbow, scolding him with her eyes for shouting after the unpleasant woman.

"I'm just curious what's inside," whispered Jasper. "Let's just take a look at what's in there and then leave. We came all this way to see the inside, didn't we?"

Regina and Joey weren't fond of the idea, but they nodded anyway, agreeing to tour the inside of the mountain with Jasper.

"I knew you were smart," said the Red Queen with a twinkle in her eye as she dramatically turned back around. "You all have potential. Come and see what Mount Napharata has to offer you." She lifted her hand mysteriously summon them forward with her index finger.

Regina, Joey and Jasper followed her as she turned around and led them through the opening in the black mountain.

Regina stared at the back of the Red Queen's black dress as they made their way through the dark tunnel. The warm light of the torches on the wall bounced back from the water-like material that flowed on her body, reminding Regina of the dark sea outside.

Her feet were not visible under the long material either, but her steps didn't sound peculiar at all. Regina was almost sure that she was wearing stilettos, probably blood red ones like her nails.

As Regina was staring at the mesmerizing movements of the Red Queen's dress, the woman suddenly stopped in front of her. Regina stopped just in time to avoid bumping into her.

"You are now inside Mount Napharata," the Red Queen said approvingly as she turned around to face them. "Only the best of the best make it here, I hope you all are aware of that."

Regina noticed that the Red Queen always looked at Jasper and her when she was talking, but never at Joey. She seemed to avoid him since she first took a look at him.

"Take a look around!" she continued as she raised her arms and spun around. "This is where the future leaders of the world are made."

Regina stepped out from behind the Red Queen, and as she looked around, she quickly realized that they were inside a volcano. The inside of the mountain was hollow, with a rock spiral staircase on the wall leading up to the opening on the very top. Holes that looked like caves were all around the wall, and could be entered from the stairs. There was no solid ground at the center of the mountain's base, only a pool of some kind of glowing red liquid, possibly lava.

For the most part, Mount Napharata looked like an active volcano. Regina only saw one thing out of the ordinary, besides the fact that the caves seemed to be inhabited, and that was the glowing red vein-like formations all over the wall of the mountain, which connected in the large pool of what looked like lava at the bottom. It looked like the glowing red liquid powered the mountain somehow. Regina also noticed that the vein-like formations touched every single cave.

"Is this the other camp?" Jasper asked, looking at the caves.

"Yes," answered the Red Queen with pride. "Isn't it wonderful?" She paused a bit to admire the mountain with an amazed look on her face.

"Can we take a look around?" Jasper asked, snapping the Red Queen out of her amazed state.

"Why, of course," she said. "I see you're eager, Jasper. Very good, very good." She went around the pool of glowing red liquid, leading them to the rock staircase.

As Regina looked at the pool of what she thought was lava, Brunorth came to her mind. She wondered if he would have liked the lava, considering he was a dragon, and she really wanted to know how he would have reacted to the Red Queen. Regina was having trouble placing her, and she knew that the tiny dragon's judgment was always correct.

"This is where our members can stay," explained the Red Queen as she stopped in front of the first cave and turned towards them. "Let me take this opportunity to say something to you all. You are all special, otherwise you would not be here. You saw how many others took the easy way out and left Andara as soon as they arrived. You stayed. You can imagine how many of those who stayed were too scared to ever make the journey to Mount Napharata. You're here. You are part of the very few. Don't let it go to waste."

140

The Red Queen's look changed as she was speaking. She smiled at them with a smile that was nothing like the wicked one stretching across her face earlier. Regina saw her mother in the warm smile under the red lipstick. She felt genuine caring in the Red Queen's voice, and as Regina looked at her, she suddenly felt safe. The burning darkness of Mount Napharata changed from scary to cozy, and Regina felt that the Red Queen, despite her appearance and earlier behavior, had their best interests in mind—just like her mother.

"We won't," Regina blurted out, to Jasper and Joey's surprise.

The Red Queen gently placed her hand on top of Regina's head.

"Good," she said softly. "I know you can make the right decision."

"That's more of Joey's specialty," said Jasper. "I'm sure you're aware that he's a Naya—"

"Let's move on!" shouted the Red Queen, interrupting Jasper. "Shall we?" she added in a softer tone and turned around.

Regina became more and more certain that the Red Queen had some sort of an issue with Joey. Regina looked at the boy, who shrugged, not understanding himself what the woman's problem might have been.

The Red Queen proceeded on the long spiral staircase and the trio followed.

"This is one of our caves that is occupied by a member," she said, stopping before another hole in the wall.

"Hey, guys," a boy came to the entrance of the cave with a friendly smile on his face. "It's nice to see new faces. You will love it here." He looked at all three of them and nodded. "Yes, we need more like you here. Nice choices, Queen. You can take a look around the cave, of course."

Regina, Jasper and Joey looked inside. The space looked very similar to the huts in the Field of Cetana in terms of furniture, but the feel of the whole room was very different. The source of light was the same glowing red liquid that flowed in the vein-like formations across the mountain, and it covered the walls of the cave as well. The black material of the mountain and the glowing red liquid that illuminated the cave gave the space a much more sinister feel than those of the huts.

"What is this red substance?" asked Jasper. "It can't be lava, can it?"

"No, Jasper, you're right as usual," said the Red Queen with a kind smile. "It's called Asantosa. It powers the whole mountain. Asantosa is a substance that is produced by people's special abilities. The more Asantosa you produce, the more it strengthens your talents. These caves help people reach their fullest potential by drawing out their Asantosa and strengthening them with it. The more special you are, the more Asantosa you will produce, and the more special you will become in the end."

"That's amazing!" said Jasper.

"It sure is," said the Red Queen. "Scientists that change the future of humanity, artists that educate ignorant hearts, and politicians that lead mankind towards a different fate are all made here. This is where special becomes one of a kind. Jasper, you have the potential in you to shape the future of mankind. And Regina, you could become an artist who reaches hearts all around the world. Don't let your potential go to waste."

"I agree," said the boy in the cave. "This place has done so much for me. I was such a lost boy when I came here. Mount Napharata has helped me find myself. I feel there's nothing I don't know now. Hey, everybody! Let's welcome the newbies!"

Different faces peeked out from every cave and they all waved at them.

"Welcome!"

"Good job, reaching the Mount!"

"You will love it here!"

Regina's stomach clenched as she listened to them. She had never felt this welcome before. Her mother's presence in her mind became stronger and stronger. Could she become the kind of person here who would make her mother proud? Could Mount Napharata be the answer to all the doubts she had about herself?

Regina's heart started pounding with the excitement of such promise. She didn't look at Jasper or Joey. She could finally become the person who she had always wanted to be—a person who was not afraid of anything, who knew what she was doing and was not looked down on. She could show her mother, her brother, and everybody who thought low of her what she was capable of.

She became so obsessed with the thought in that moment, that her surroundings started to become blurry before her eyes. She still saw the Red Queen's mouth stretch to a contented smile before she became a red and black smudge in front of her.

The sounds of the mountain became muffled, and Regina leaned against the wall to support herself. She tried to gain back her composure, but the world around her just became more and more smudged. As she tried to blink quicker to clear her vision, she noticed a large black spot emerging from the red pool at the bottom of the mountain.

No matter how hard Regina tried to clear her vision, her surroundings remained blurry, and the black spot slowly rose closer and closer to them.

She tried to look at Jasper and Joey, who seemed to be experiencing the same thing. The smudge resembling Jasper was on the stairs on all fours, and the smudge that looked like Joey was leaning against the wall as his other arm was supporting his head.

When Regina turned her head back towards the black spot, it was already floating in front of them. As it moved, it looked like someone taking a black hood off a bald head. Regina realized that the threatening spot in front of them must have been a person or some kind of Andarian creature, and she could still make out that the Red Queen was bowing before it.

She wanted to move away, but her body was not

responding. She stood there helplessly, staring at the blurry scene, and she still saw two spots, where the black creature's eyes should have been, starting to glow with a red light before a completely different world appeared in front of her eyes.

Her mom was standing in front of her, smiling.

"I'm so proud of you, Regina," she said as tears sneaked in her eyes. "Even your father came to see you."

She stepped aside, and Regina saw a long red curtain appear in the light. She stepped towards it, and the curtain suddenly rose, revealing a large and elegant audience, who stood up in standing ovation as Regina appeared before them. Regina looked back at her mother, who was also clapping as tears were streaming down her face.

A podium with a shiny gold trophy on it broke the smoothness of the stage. Regina reached for the sparkling statue of a star and read the large black text written across it: *Regina White, Generation Award.*

Regina looked at the clapping crowd and saw her father in the first row, who was now accompanied by her mother. He was smiling, and he winked at Regina when their eyes met.

"Dad . . ." Regina's eyes were flooded with tears.

She did it—she made everybody proud and happy. She surveyed the crowd and saw many unfamiliar faces. She didn't know anybody besides her parents. They all kept clapping and smiling, and as Regina took a closer look at their faces, they seemed strangely stiff and motionless.

As the standing ovation continued and became even louder, Regina noticed that her parents were talking to her, but she couldn't hear a word they were saying because of the clapping.

She jumped off the stage and tried to approach her parents, but as she stepped closer to them, the dimensions changed, and suddenly the crowd seemed to be farther away from her. She tried to reach towards them, but the more she approached them, the farther they got.

She despairingly tried to run towards them, but there was no use. She broke down on the red carpet, and as she collapsed, she dropped the award on the floor. She was breathing heavily, and as she was kneeling on the ground, she desperately watched the emotionless crowd continue to clap with their stiff smiles stretched across their faces.

She looked at the shiny statue on the floor and tears appeared in her eyes. She put her head between her knees on the floor and covered her ears with her hands.

The gold award on the posh red carpet looked pathetic to her in that moment, but it seemed to be her only companion.

As she lay on the floor, enduring the noise of the clapping crowd, Agnitio popped into her mind. He had said that he could help anytime, anywhere.

An unusual feeling took over her all of a sudden. She felt a surge of confidence flow through her out of seemingly nowhere.

She stood up and took a last look at the shiny award

before she kicked it out of her sight. The clapping suddenly stopped and all the unfamiliar faces disappeared, revealing other people, ones Regina couldn't see before: Joey, Jasper and Snow were smiling at her from different points in the audience. Only they and her parents occupied the audience space now.

Regina smiled at them and they all smiled back at her. Regina felt at peace in the quiet room and didn't feel the need to say anything. The silent smiles of these few filled the room more than the empty claps of the crowd.

As she took a deep breath, appreciating the serenity of the moment, the large room started to disappear into a bright white light before her eyes. The whole picture in front of her was swallowed by the light, and just when all she could see was whiteness, she felt herself opening her eyes.

She was lying on her back. She was not inside Mount Napharata anymore, the clear blue sky was above her once again.

Closer than the Andarian sky, a new face was smiling above her. An enchantingly pale face surrounded by snow white hair, with light blue, almost white, eyes. The beautiful woman exuded more kindness and love than Regina had ever felt before.

"You did it, Regina," she said in a soft and gentle voice. "I'm proud of you."

10: SEPARATE WAYS

Regina was mesmerized by the beauty of the woman in front of her. Her pale skin, white hair, light eyes and long white dress gave the impression she was glowing with an otherworldly light.

For a short while, Regina didn't even think about where she was, and how she might have gotten there, she was so submerged in the beauty the woman exuded, but suddenly the sound of waves crashing crawled into her ears.

Snapped out of her enchantment, Regina sat up and turned her head away from the beautiful woman. She immediately realized she was on a ship. The vessel looked like it was made of ice, but since it was not cold, Regina thought it might have been a crystal ship.

The light of the sun bounced back from the beautiful raw crystal formations everywhere on the ship. The soft wind was pushing the vessel forward as the two crystal sails collected the breeze.

As Regina looked around, the absence of her friends overshadowed the beauty around her.

"Excuse me, but where's Jasper and Joey?" she asked politely, but with concern in her voice.

"Don't worry, Regina, they're both all right," said the woman, her voice smooth as air. "Joey is below deck, he's resting. The encounter with Bellator was a bit more straining for him as a Nayaka, but he'll be fine."

"And Jasper?" Regina asked with hesitation, fearing the answer.

"Jasper's choice differed from yours," said the woman calmly.

Regina's stomach clenched.

"What does that mean?" she asked.

"Jasper made his own choice, Regina," said the woman with sympathy in her eyes.

"But he made the wrong choice!" Regina shouted as tears gathered in her eyes.

She stood up and ran to the crystal railing of the ship. She looked back at the dark spot on the horizon that was Mount Napharata. Jasper couldn't have decided to stay in that horrible mountain, there must have been some kind of misunderstanding.

As she was desperately looking at the black smudge, trying to think of ways to bring Jasper back, a blurry image of a cloaked man flashed before her eyes like a static picture of a maladjusted television set.

Regina shook her head, and the image was gone.

"It might be the wrong choice in your eyes, but Jasper's eyes see a different world than yours." The woman stepped next to Regina and rested her pale hands on the railing. "For him, it was the right choice to make."

Regina heard Astraea's words, but her mind was too occupied to understand them. *What is happening? Did I go crazy? Is this my punishment for not staying in Mount Napharata? Did I make a bad choice?*

"He'll have lots of chances to turn around, you know," said the woman, gazing at the dark spot on the horizon. "One choice does not define a whole fate."

It doesn't define a whole fate. Regina repeated the sentence in her head, but it was like the words had lost all meaning—her mind was unable to understand them, and now a dangerously huge ball of anxiety started growing in her stomach.

The glowingly beautiful woman looked at Regina, and she

understood the situation in an instant, it seemed. She didn't say anything, she just put her soft palm on top of Regina's head.

Regina's every distress ended in that moment. Her mind was empty and calm, and the raging tension in her body died down as well.

"You must be wondering how you got here," said the woman after a couple of minutes. Her voice was gentle, almost like a whisper.

"Hmm?" Regina turned to look at the woman like she was just woken from relaxing sleep, and the woman let her hand down from Regina's head with a heartwarmingly gentle smile.

"My name is Astraea, and as you were witnessing Bellator's illusion, you and Joey called for me."

"We called for you?" Regina's mind was still slow to process the words, but now because of its relaxed state.

Astraea pointed at Regina's chest. Her long pale finger glowed in the sunlight.

"Your heart called for me," she said.

She gently stroked Regina's cheek with her fingers, which felt like warm silk against Regina's skin.

"I am the last stage here in Andara, and not everybody makes it to me. That makes you very important."

"Important?" Regina's brain slowly started working again.

"Some, ones like your friend, Jasper, are unable to see me. For them, Mount Napharata remains the last destination when they accept Bellator as their queen."

151

"Jasper couldn't see you?"

"No, he couldn't," said Astraea. "You see, anger is like a blindfold. It hides your hurt and fear from the world, but it also makes you blind. People who cannot see are easy to fool. That's what Bellator and Ate use to their advantage as they create their army. Only those who are brave enough to let go of their own emotions cannot be fooled." She paused for a moment and smiled at Regina. "You were brave enough."

I was brave enough? But . . . I'm not brave at all. This must be some kind of mistake. This was what Regina thought, but what she said out loud was simply, "Oh. I see."

"What really creates Asantosa, the red liquid in Mount Napharata, is people's discontent. Bellator and Ate use it to power the whole mountain and make Ate stronger. They make people believe that they could become more, that they could become better, but all they really do is feed people's discontent, therefor giving more power to Ate. What a lot of humans fail to see is that they don't need to do anything to be valuable—they already are."

Regina felt sadness overcome her as she thought about Jasper lying in one of the caves in Mount Napharata.

"Don't feel sorry for them," said Astraea. "Every moment is a chance to turn around. However small, hope always remains."

A noise sounded from behind Regina. She turned around and saw Joey emerging from below deck. Regina was so happy to see at least one familiar face that she ran towards

152

Joey and gave him a big hug.

"Glad to see you're okay," said Joey, his face turning tomato-red. He hugged Regina back casually with one arm.

"How are you doing?" Regina asked with concern as she let go of the boy.

"I'm better now. The Red Queen gave me a pretty bad headache, but it's almost completely gone now."

"A headache?" asked Regina. "How come?"

"I'm not sure." Joey turned his head towards Astraea.

"I'm glad to hear you're better." Astraea walked towards them, smiling, with her long white hair flowing in the wind. "You experienced a headache because your body responded to Bellator trying to turn you against your Nayaka nature. By the way, did you notice that she was treating you differently?"

"Yes, she didn't even look at me," said Joey.

"She couldn't face you," said Astraea. "Did you sense anything about her?"

"Well," said Joey, trying to think back, "I just felt a kind of . . . pity towards her, I guess."

"Yes, pity." Astraea nodded. "Joey, you and Bellator have something in common: Bellator was also a Nayaka once."

"Really?" Joey's eyes widened in surprise.

"But how is that possible?" Regina couldn't believe her ears.

"I assume you remember Y'sis telling you that the heart of a Nayaka is the purest of them all. The pure are the most easily tainted. A Nayaka's heart usually prevails, in fact,

Bellator is the only Nayaka who lost the battle with her own anger. She is the first and only Danava, a Nayaka whose soul turned black. May there never be more."

Regina and Joey listened to what Astraea said with their mouths slightly open from surprise.

"Y'sis told us that one Nayaka turned into a Danava," said Regina, "but she didn't tell us it was the Red Queen."

"You needed to meet her without prejudice," Astraea explained.

"How did she become like this?" asked Joey with a saddened look on his face.

"People are often led astray by what they think they need. When thoughts overshadow the heart is when people make bad choices."

"Can she still change back?" asked Regina.

"The deeper you sink in darkness, the harder it becomes to turn your head back, but it's never impossible," said Astraea. "A small spark always remains glistening in the heart."

Astraea placed her hands on Regina's and Joey's shoulders.

"Your hearts couldn't be led astray," she said. "The love you hold in it is far greater than any earthly desire, and that which is done out of love goes beyond good and evil. Remember that, and be proud of your heart. It's your greatest treasure."

Regina heard Astraea's words, but her mind was too occupied to understand them. Astraea gently let go of their shoulders, and Regina's eyes wandered to the horizon again. Since she and Jasper started school together, they were always very close friends, and Regina had always felt that she was able to help Jasper when he got swallowed by his anger. The fact that he was not there with her on the crystal ship felt like a failure to Regina, and she couldn't think about anything else.

It's my fault. I'm such a bad person. I don't belong here. I don't belong anywhere.

An image of her brother flashed before Regina's eyes, uninvited again.

"Regina, seriously, you are so stupid," the intrusive picture said.

Regina closed her eyes and shook her head, but only a new image took the last one's place this time.

"Don't interrupt, little girl, the big men are talking." Clive's voice forced itself into Regina's mind accompanied by the large boy's blurry picture.

"You just don't get him." Snow's face protruded into Regina's vision, her voice echoing in her mind, shutting everything else out.

What is happening? No, no, no, no. Make it stop. I can't see. I can't see.

"I—" Regina tried to ask for help, but the words only came out as gibberish from her mouth.

What's happening? Am I dying? I must be dying. I shouldn't have stayed here. I should have just went home. I'm such a failure. This is what I get for being such an idiot.

155

Every image left Regina's mind, and only one remained. The picture of the cloaked man. His face was covered by his black hood. The image was not blurry this time, it was crystal clear. He held out his hand towards Regina. His fingers were like bones. Gray like the dead.

He was only a vision, but Regina could have sworn she smelled his stench. The smell of ashes and burnt meat.

I don't want to touch you, I don't . . .

"Do you have a choice?" A voice echoed in Regina's mind unlike anything she had ever heard before. A voice that was definitely not human, but still strangely comprehensible.

Maybe I don't . . .

The cloaked figure floated closer and closer to Regina, his deathly fingers almost touching her.

No . . .

Regina tried to wiggle away from the disgusting hand. Suddenly, her view turned upside down, and the scary creature slid out of it like a piece of paper floating away in the wind, and Regina felt like she was falling. When she had landed, the only thing she felt was warmth.

Did I really die?

Regina's eyes now only saw whiteness. She blinked a couple of times. She could see clearly again. No more intrusive images.

She was lying on the ground, but on something soft and fluffy.

A cloud? I really am dead.

"Are you two okay? It's just snow." Astraea's voice was like a gentle caress.

Regina sat up. The crystal ship had docked, and Regina had somehow fallen off of it, right onto an island of, apparently, warm snow.

"What the—" Joey spoke somewhere near her, and soon after, Regina saw him sitting up about seven feet away from her. His face looked like he had just woken up with a migraine.

"You too, Joey?" Regina felt a little better knowing that she wasn't alone in what she had just experienced.

"Everything's all right," said Astraea, like what had happened to them was something commonplace.

"I know it's hard to believe right now, but this is actually a good thing." Astraea walked towards Regina and helped her up from the ground. "This is the Island of Pyara. My home. Welcome."

"So, we're not dead?" asked Regina, feeling dizzy standing on her feet.

"No, you're not." Astraea smiled and helped Joey get on his feet as well. "On the contrary actually."

Regina turned around, and the view in front of her eyes was the most beautiful she had ever seen. A large castle stood in the middle of the small island. It looked like it was made out of the same material as the ship, and the land around it was covered in snow, which was softly falling from the clear sky. The sun's rays sparkled brightly on every single snowflake.

Regina's mouth curved to a slight smile at the sight of the wondrous place, but the uneasy feeling in her stomach made her gather her brows instead.

She felt like she had just gotten off the world's largest roller coaster, and Regina didn't like roller coasters one bit.

She lifted her right hand to her mouth, and grew very conscious of the fact that she was feeling horrible in a place far away from her home. She was light-headed, her stomach hurt, her steps were heavy. She suddenly craved the comfort of the solitary little fort that was her bedroom.

"There is something on this island only the rare few who make it here can take a look into." Astraea stood on the snow, in front of the beautiful castle, and the whole scene looked like a magical snow globe.

Regina couldn't enjoy what lay before her though—her aches overshadowed everything else.

"Regina, Joey, come this way." Astraea turned around and began walking towards the castle.

Regina felt like a large pot of water was boiling inside of her stomach, ready to spill.

"I'm sorry, I can't," she said, blurting out the words, and turned around, walking away from Astraea and Joey. She couldn't bear to see anyone in that moment. She didn't even care about the rare magical whatever they could look into. She just wanted to be alone. She had had enough of everything.

Astraea and Joey didn't say a word, at least Regina didn't hear.

It had all gotten too much for Regina. In a blink of an eye, her friend had been taken by a discontent-sucking army of weirdoes, who were planning who knows what, and she couldn't do anything to help him. She couldn't do anything to help him, ever. And now these abnormal visions would keep haunting her forever, probably making her crazy. She should have just went back home before any of this happened.

She didn't care about what Astraea had to show them, because Regina didn't feel like she deserved any special treatment. She didn't feel good about herself, she didn't even feel adequate. And on top of all of that, she was physically in pain too.

She crouched down in the warm snow, eyes narrow. The sunlight on the whiteness was not doing any favors for her light head.

She took a scoop of the snow. It felt more like a cloud. As the little flakes rained between her fingers, she raised her head. The black smudge of Mount Napharata was still visible on the horizon. Regina plopped onto the ground. Her blinks were slow and heavy. Nothing could be done. Absolutely nothing.

Just for a fraction of a second, the cloaked figure intruded into her mind again, blocking out everything else, but Regina didn't have any emotion left to give. Her body couldn't have tensed up more either. She could just go home. All she had to do was wish it.

"It will help, the mirror." Astraea had walked next to

159

Regina, and her voice was as gentle as the weakest summer breeze. "Trust me."

Regina glanced at Astraea without turning her head. Her voice sounded strangely familiar to her, and it brought back a feeling she had felt long ago—a pleasant feeling of an old friendship.

Regina turned to look up at Astraea, who was smiling the kindest smile Regina had ever seen.

Regina nodded and got up from the ground. The commotion in her body eased a little from Astraea's presence, but it was far from gone.

Astraea put her arm around Regina. Her pale arms were soft and warm, just like the snow.

She gently led Regina to the castle. As they walked through the crystal gates, something felt oddly familiar to Regina again. Like a protective mother was guiding her home.

Joey was already standing inside the castle. The interior was spacious and bright, with only one item inside—a beautiful crystal frame on the wall. At first glance it looked empty, only containing the piece of crystal wall behind it, but as Regina looked more carefully, she noticed small droplets moving downwards inside of it. Almost like it encompassed a small waterfall.

Regina and Joey looked at each other for a split second. Joey looked just as worn as Regina felt.

"One at a time," said Astraea, standing next to the frame.

"Go ahead," said Joey and stepped back to make way for

Regina.

"Me?" Regina looked at Astraea. "No, you should go first." She didn't feel like she deserved going first when she didn't even want to come in.

"Okay then." Joey stepped in front of the frame.

As he looked into it, the dripping water froze, and Joey seemed to fall in some kind of trance. He just stood there staring at the frozen droplets, but Regina couldn't see a thing inside the frame besides the frozen water.

"Is he okay?" asked Regina.

"He's fine," Astraea replied. "There aren't many things better than looking into the Mirror of Saccai."

"What is he seeing?"

"You will have a chance to see for yourself soon," said Astraea with a smile.

Regina scanned Joey's face. His eyes looked like they were madly looking at something that wasn't actually there. After a couple of minutes, Regina noticed that his eyes began filling up with tears.

"What's happening?" Regina asked with worry.

"Those aren't tears of sadness," said Astraea.

Joey suddenly shook his head, and as he closed his eyes, the blink pushed the tears onto his cheeks. He quickly wiped them away, and an emotional smile appeared on his face. His fatigue was gone.

The droplets inside the frame unfroze and started flowing again.

"Wow," he said, his voice shaking. He appeared to be

wanting to say something, but he couldn't find the words.

Regina had already noticed that, unlike her, the boy's main way of communicating was not through his words.

"Thank you, Astraea," he said finally, after realizing he couldn't possibly form words out of what he was feeling.

Astraea smiled at him and nodded.

"Regina," Joey said, turning towards her, "you have to take a look too."

Regina, unable to imagine what Joey must have seen in the frame, questioningly looked at Astraea. Astraea nodded with encouragement.

Joey stepped next to Astraea, and Regina hesitantly stepped in his place. She kept her eyes where the wall met the floor, avoiding looking into the frame. She took one last look at Joey, who smiled and nodded at her.

The aches in Regina's body seemed less unsettling now. The atmosphere in the crystal castle was like home.

She smiled back then looked into the frame.

The water droplets froze immediately when she looked at them. She blinked, but when she opened her eyes again, she was no longer standing in the crystal palace.

11. INSIDE THE MIRROR

Regina was standing in what looked like a school.

The crowds of students rushing from one classroom to another formed a blur before her eyes. Among the faded silhouettes of many, however, Regina could see three people clearly. She started to walk towards them, stepping through the blurred crowd of students with ease, and she realized that no one there could see or hear her. She was like air in this unusual scene she had been dropped into.

As she got closer to the group of three, she noticed that they were arguing. A thin boy was being pushed around by two larger boys. Regina didn't recognize either of them.

"Why are you hitting yourself?" said one of the large boys, slapping the thin boy's face with his own hand while the other boy laughed.

The two large boys seemed unnecessarily cruel to Regina, and the slim boy helpless. She looked around, but no one in the blurred crowd had stopped to help, no one even looked their way. The group of three seemed to be invisible to the hectic smudge that was the rest of the school.

163

Just when Regina felt like she couldn't watch any longer, a voice echoed through the blur of the crowd.

"Leave him alone!" the voice shouted. A girl broke through the crowd and ran towards them. "Leave him alone!" she repeated as she grabbed the thin boy and pulled him away from the other two.

The large boy let go of him, and the laughing stopped as well. The girl protectively pushed the thin boy behind herself.

"You make no sense, just leave him alone!"

The two large boys acted like they didn't even hear her, turned around and left the scene. As they walked away, they blended into the blur of the crowd.

Regina breathed a sigh of relief. She thought the girl was brave, heroic and just plain awesome. Someone she would have liked to have as a friend. The thin boy seemed to be relieved as well.

"Thank you," he said, smiling gratefully at the girl, "Regina."

The unknown faces of the girl and the boy suddenly became familiar to Regina's eyes—it was her and Jasper. Suddenly, it all became clear to her, and she remembered that this was not an illusion—it was a memory.

Regina's eyes suddenly got flushed with tears as she watched herself and Jasper smile at each other.

"It's all right, buddy," her past self said to Jasper as she playfully put her arm around his shoulder.

The two friends smilingly walked into the blur of the

crowd and disappeared. Regina's tears were now washing her cheeks as she pushed her shaking lips together. The brave, heroic and just plain awesome girl was her.

After her next blink, she was standing in the crystal palace. Her head felt right again. She was not dizzy and light-headed anymore, and no part of her body was in pain.

Regina couldn't find the words to say.

"How was it?" Astraea asked kindly.

Regina bit her upper lip and nodded a couple of times.

"I'm glad you chose to take a look at it in the end." Being looked upon by Astraea felt like a comfortable embrace.

"I'm sorry," said Regina. "I don't know what came over me."

"It's all right," said Astraea. "It's natural, what you went through. It's what will make you strong. You don't have to be afraid of it."

"Will it . . . continue happening?" asked Joey, confirming that he had experienced the same—the intrusive images.

"It might arise sometimes. It might not. The first time is always the toughest. But it can never overpower you if you don't give it power yourself. Never forget that."

Astraea stepped between Regina and Joey and hugged them both.

"Come on then, it's time to go back," she said.

She let go of them and walked out the castle. Her long dress glided behind her on the crystal floor, the sun reflecting from every part of her white frame.

Regina and Joey followed her out of the castle. They were

walking through the warm winter wonderland when one large pile of snow suddenly started moving, scaring Regina so much that she tripped on her own feet and almost fell over.

"Astraea, why is the snow moving?" she asked, not wanting to pass the moving snow pile.

Astraea turned around to see what Regina was talking about. The surprised look on her face quickly turned into a soft smile.

"That's not snow," she said, laughing gently. "That's Asa. Stop being silly, Asa, come out of there."

Regina and Joey watched as the large white ball became even bigger and slowly revealed itself to be a breathtakingly beautiful white horse with glimmering white wings on its back.

Regina and Joey were speechless. They stared at the wonderful creature that was about two times as large as a regular horse with amazement.

Astraea chuckled and walked back to them. The creature dutifully lowered its head, and Astraea touched the pegasus' snout with her palm.

"Asa, you almost forgot to say hello to Regina and Joey."

The pegasus carefully turned towards Regina and Joey and respectfully lowered its head and wings.

"He is honored to meet you," Astraea translated the creature's body language. "He wants me to tell you the story of the black pegasus you saw at Mount Napharata." Astraea lowered her head, and a tint of sadness appeared in her eyes.

"Devol, the black pegasus you saw, was once living with us here on the Island of Pyara. She was dear friends with Asa, they were inseparable. She was also sparkling white once, like Asa."

Astraea paused for a moment and raised her head to look at the creature. The pegasus' light blue eyes told the story of heartache. The sadness Regina recognized in them was familiar and all too human.

Regina stepped towards him and compassionately petted his snout. Asa closed his eyes.

"One day," Astraea continued, "Devol started acting differently. She seemed discontent with her life on the island and began wanting something else, something more. That was when the dark spots first appeared on her. Pegasi are unsteady creatures, they are easily swallowed by darkness if they are not careful. The black spots slowly took over her body and one day, she was gone." Astraea looked at Asa apologetically for tearing up the old wound that was the loss of his friend.

"We still see her sometimes, roaming over Mount Napharata. We still hope for her return. Change is a difficult choice, but it's always possible. I believe that our sweet Devol will return one day, happier than ever before."

Regina felt her heart tighten inside her chest. Jasper came to her mind.

The sadness was overthrown by a kind smile on Astraea's face. She stepped next to Asa and gently stroked his long white mane. The pegasus opened his eyes and playfully glanced at Astraea.

"You have seen everything that was needed to be seen here on the Island of Pyara," said Astraea. "Listen, Regina, Joey. When dark skies will be above you, remember to be the light yourselves. The ones who reach the Island of Pyara hold great responsibility. It's in their hands the fate of the world rests."

"What do you mean?" asked Regina, struck by the weight of Astraea's words.

"I mean the fate of both this world and the other. You are what can light up the darkness."

"I don't understand," said Joey, confused himself. "What should we do?"

Astraea smiled and gently put her hands on their heads.

"Nothing. Just be."

Regina gathered her brows. Just being didn't sound like a great way to handle such a responsibility.

"Now that Asa has decided to show himself," said Astraea, lowering her hands from their heads and dropping the serious topic, "he can take you back to the Field of Cetana. Isn't that right, Asa?" Astraea softly patted the pegasus on the back, and Asa snorted with excitement.

"Do you mean," said Joey with a bit of fear in his voice, "on his back?"

"Of course," said Astraea, and Asa gently kneeled before Regina and Joey.

"I'm a little afraid of heights," Joey admitted quietly.

"What an amazing chance to overcome a fear then!"

replied Astraea.

The expression on Joey's face told he was not exactly comforted by Astraea's reply.

"This is where we part. Seeing you again warmed my heart. Have fun in Andara, dear friends." Astraea smiled at them with her inimitable smile and stepped away from the kneeling pegasus.

Regina felt too shy to thank her, so she tried to smile at her as gratefully as she could and then climbed on Asa's back. Joey did the same and sat in front of Regina. The pegasus straightened up, and Joey grabbed his mane.

The creature opened his wings and pushed himself away from the ground. Regina couldn't find anything to grab onto as the pegasus ascended into the sky, so she grabbed Joey's waist. She was glad the boy couldn't see her blushing face, and that he was probably more occupied with his fear of heights.

As Asa flew higher, Regina kept her eyes on Astraea, who slowly disappeared below the warm snowflakes flying through the air. Regina felt a tiny bit of sadness in her heart as the Island of Pyara disappeared from her eyes, but she didn't have much time to wallow in sorrow, because Asa charged forward. Regina instinctually grabbed tighter onto Joey's waist, and when she realized what she was forced to do, even more blood rushed into her face.

When she got over her embarrassment, she looked at the scenery before her. They were flying over the sea—the snowflakes were gone, and Regina could see the light blue sky and sea clearly. The many sparkling stars seemed even brighter from up there.

Asa flew smoothly through the comfortably warm air with the gentle flap of his wings.

"This is amazing!" Joey exclaimed joyfully.

Regina was glad Joey had gotten over his fear and was enjoying himself. After a couple of minutes of peaceful flying, the green grass of the Field of Cetana appeared below them, and the thatched roofs of the huts emerged as well.

The pegasus slowly began descending and gently landed on the grass. He kneeled down, and Regina and Joey got off his back.

"Thanks, Asa," said Joey.

Regina bowed her head before the creature in gratitude. The pegasus softly neighed, opened his wings and pushed himself up from the soft grass of the Field of Cetana. Regina and Joey watched as he disappeared between the stars. When they couldn't see him anymore, Joey turned towards Regina.

"Well, we're back," he said, looking around.

Regina looked over to the huts. A few people were walking among them, looking around probably for the first time. They were too far to see the pegasus that had just descended from the sky. Regina wondered if she had also missed Asa when she was first wandering around the huts, shouting at the flowers and deciding to stay in Andara.

"We're back. The field is still the same," she said to Joey. "But we are not."

Joey looked at her silently. He was clearly not used to Regina's dramatic statements yet.

"I mean that in a good way!" Regina tried to explain herself quickly.

Joey nodded.

The sun was going down, and its warm rays painted the starry Andarian horizon orange, pink and purple. Regina and Joey watched the sunset in silence for a while.

"Are you glad you stayed?" Regina broke the silence in a softer voice than usual.

"I am," said Joey.

They didn't take their eyes off the colorful sky as they spoke.

"Do you think it's better to see all of this stuff than to just . . . go home and not see?" asked Regina.

Joey swallowed.

"I think it's different," he answered.

They had started their journey as a group of four, including tiny Brunorth, and only Joey was next to Regina now. *What could Jasper be doing right now?* The sunset they were watching was not even visible from Mount Napharata. *Jasper's eyes see a different world.*

The sun's rays disappeared from the horizon, and only the stars were shining their light on the land now.

"Do you want to come with me to my hut?" asked Joey, but he immediately continued, "Oh, no, that sounded so wrong, I mean . . ."

Regina chuckled at the embarrassed boy.

"I know what you mean, don't worry. Sure, let's go."

They began walking in the soft grass that was still warm from the rays of the now sleeping sun. The bright stars of Andara lit their way. The tiny white flowers called Fairypalms peeping out from the grass were all closed up, indicating the end of the day. Only the sound of their feet on the grass could be heard as they were walking next to each other in silence.

Most of the huts they passed were empty, but the light of the Dragontears beaconed through one or two windows, signaling people inside who had decided to stay.

As they walked past these lit up huts, Regina felt happy that some people had chosen to stay. When she noticed her own joy, she realized that she, too, must have made the right choice in staying.

12. UNDER THE NIGHT SKY

Joey's hut was cozy and inviting, even though it looked almost exactly the same as Regina's. They didn't spend much time inside of it though, because they made themselves some tea, grabbed a couple different fruits from the jars in the cupboards and sat outside of the hut. They leaned against the wall of the hut as they were enjoying the satisfying beverages and fruits. Millions of stars were shining above them in the black sky, and no sound disrupted the peace of the land at all.

"You didn't even tell me how you got to Andara yet," said Joey, his voice quiet and soft, almost like a whisper. Nothing more was needed in the unbroken silence.

"Well, I was coming home from school one day." Regina placed the warm mug of tea in her lap. "It was already dark out."

"Dark out? Why were you at school so late?"

"I like reading in the library. Sometimes it's better to be there than home."

"Oh." Joey sighed. "I can relate to that."

173

Regina nodded. She knew the boy understood what she was talking about more than anybody else.

"So, I was on my way home, and I heard horse hooves in one of the dark alleys I was passing. And I mean dark as in pitch black. I couldn't see anything, so I thought a horse was trapped in there or something. I love animals a lot, so I went in to help, and well, you know the rest—it was Agnitio, not a horse."

"That's funny." Joey took a bite of the apple-looking fruit in his hand. "It's so weird to imagine Agnitio in Tupsbade just wandering in random alleys."

"Abducting unsuspecting children." Regina pulled a scary face, and they both laughed out loud.

"You already told me how you got here," Regina said after their laughing died down, "so I'm not going to ask again. It must be hard to talk about these things. You sleeping on a bench and all."

"It hasn't been hard, because I never spoke about them. Listen, Regina . . . I want to thank you for . . . you know . . . not turning your back on me after you found out . . . you know . . . that newspaper clipping in Eris' castle."

Regina waved her arm. She was a little embarrassed the boy felt like he needed to thank her for something she considered ordinary.

"Come on, Joey," she said, "you don't have to thank me. That's what normal people do."

"Well, I don't know what's normal where you come from, but that's definitely not normal for me."

Regina averted her eyes from Joey to look at the ground and smiled.

"You're welcome then," she said.

They both looked up at the stars in silence.

"Eris was a real butt," Regina said suddenly.

Joey burst out laughing, and Regina joined in too.

When their laughing subsided, Joey began to think aloud: "I wonder why he hasn't been banished like the rest of the Living Dead."

"Agnitio said something about it being important to see who you don't want to become or something like that," said Regina, looking at Joey. "It worked on me, that's for sure. I used to obsess over violent crimes, wanting to understand why people commit them. I know now that nothing's black and white. There's a whole life story behind every action."

Joey let his head rest against the wall of the hut and gazed up at the stars as he took another bite of the fruit. A few locks of his black hair were scattered over his face. Regina took a sip of her warm tea as she averted her eyes from the boy, and she looked up at the stars again.

"I wonder if we really have the freedom to choose who we become," said Joey, continuing to wonder. It seemed the quiet and calm atmosphere had brought out a side of him Regina had not seen before. "You don't have to tell me if you don't want to, but what did you see outside Eris' castle when you looked at the wall?"

Regina's stomach clenched just thinking about the bitter old woman who disdainfully stared back at her from the glossy black wall like Regina was the most despicable person she had ever seen.

"I saw someone I don't want to become," she answered, avoiding details.

"Oh . . . I guess we all saw the same then."

"Did you see yourself as a Danava?" Regina looked at Joey.

"Yeah, I guess it was that. It was not pretty."

"Do you think it's possible that we will become those people?"

"Everything is possible, I think that's what Andara is trying to tell us."

Regina looked up at the stars again and didn't say anything for a couple of minutes.

"What could have Jasper seen?" she asked, breaking her silence.

Joey didn't answer immediately.

"Probably something that was more real to him that what we've seen," he said finally.

Regina's stomach clenched again, but her eyes didn't have any more tears to cry.

"I never thought he would ever make a choice like that," she said.

"I know what you mean. I never understood my mom's choices either."

The world felt like it had paused under the sparkling black sky, and all the chaos in the universe had gone to sleep. The darkness of the world could not touch them in that moment.

"I guess we can only be responsible for our own choices," said Regina. "We have no say in what other's choose to do at the end of the day."

"Yeah," agreed Joey, still peacefully gazing at the stars. "It's easier said than done though."

"It's better to love someone and have to deal with these stuff than to not love anyone at all, I think."

Joey didn't reply, but Regina saw from the corner of her eye that he was smiling.

"So, what's it like being a Nayaka?"

"I'm starting to come to terms with it. First, when Y'sis told me this whole story, I didn't really believe it. I was so convinced all my life that I was simply a bad person, some kind of evil psycho maybe. I still think sometimes that I might be dreaming right now, and I'll wake up one day in some kind of strait-jacket or something, and I'll be telling the nurses to let me go, because I'm a Nayaka, the deer girl told me so." Joey realized how absurd his thoughts were when he had said them out loud and laughed.

"I assure you, it's all real," Regina said with a smile. "Either that or I'm in the padded cell next to yours right now."

They both laughed.

"Did you also see some sort of illusion in Mount Napharata?" asked Regina.

"You mean when that cloaked person ascended from the lava?"

"Yeah, the same one that forced himself into our minds uninvited."

"I'm guessing he was that Lord Ate the Red Queen kept talking about. I saw an illusion too, yeah, it was actually pretty frightening, now that I think about it," said Joey and scratched his head.

Regina didn't want to ask about what Joey had seen, mainly because she didn't want to talk about her own illusion.

They enjoyed the comfortable silence for a little while, then Regina said, "So, are you feeling better about . . . you know, about what happened to your dad?"

"Well, I'm still not the violent type to be honest. I don't think I'll be using the curse aspect of this whole Nayaka thing. At least I'll try my best to avoid it. But if I wouldn't have done what I did . . . it would have ended a lot worse. I see now that I did the right thing. Screw what everybody else thinks, right?"

"Right," said Regina and turned her head again to smile at him.

She was glad to see the boy so confident after witnessing how he used to be. She thought Joey deserved to be at peace with himself more than anyone.

"What do you think happened to the Red Queen that turned her into a Danava?" Joey asked suddenly.

"Well, I'm not sure. It must have been something pretty traumatic though. To make a Nayaka turn . . . I can't even imagine."

Joey didn't say anything, so Regina looked at him and quickly added: "I'm sure you will never turn into a Danava. You're the kindest person ever, seriously."

Joey laughed out loud.

"What?" Regina asked with a smile. "You are!"

They both laughed for about a minute. The dark and silent land came alive with their sound.

"What do you think will happen next?" Joey asked after gathering his breath. "Now that we're back here."

"I don't know," replied Regina, and the realization that they might have to go home very soon descended upon her chest.

"Agnitio said that most people go home after about a month, so we still have plenty of time before we'll be considered Living Dead material," said Joey, probably because he saw the saddened expression on Regina's face.

"Maybe I can become an anti-example and get a little castle here with all sorts of good books," said Regina. "I wouldn't mind that actually."

Joey laughed and then said, "I wouldn't mind that either."

They sat next to each other silently for a short while as they watched the dark sky sparkling and enjoyed the rest of their fruits and tea.

"Do you remember what Eris said?" Regina asked after they finished eating and drinking.

"What do you mean?"

"What he said about pushing us over the line. And those glass bubbles he had . . . Do you think he's watching us right now?"

They looked at each other with concern.

"He might be, I mean . . . he can see everything in Andara, right?" said Joey.

"Everything he's interested in, yeah. I still don't get why he's allowed here. I mean, I get that he's an anti-example, but still. He's allowed to spy on everybody and then try to provoke us? Even Agnitio seemed concerned when he was talking about him."

"Maybe they consider it some kind of test for us?" Joey wondered.

"Do you think some kind of test is coming up now that we're back? That Eris will test us based on what he has observed? Could that be the darkness Astraea was talking about?"

"It might be," said Joey. "I guess it would make sense, wouldn't it?"

Regina quietly let out a long, uncomfortable squeak.

"I really don't like tests."

Joey laughed at the sight of the grumbling Regina.

"I'm sure it will be fine," he said. "This is Andara after all. And we both reached the Island of Pyara, so I think we would slay any kind of test."

Regina was calmed by Joey's words. He was right—they had reached the Island of Pyara, which was something only a small minority could say. Why did she always forget she was not as bad and useless as she thought she was?

"You're right," she said with a smile. "What about Jasper though?"

Joey couldn't answer.

"Eris seemed to tease him the most," Regina added.

"He's a good guy at heart," Joey said eventually. "I mean, I don't know him as much as you do, but I still think he's a good guy. He was very nice to me, and that's just not that common. I know how hard it is to deal with abuse every single day. It can really take a toll on a person. But I think that somewhere under all that, Jasper's a good person. I know you know that too."

If Regina had any tears left, her eyes would have become teary again. Her father was violent a couple of times before he left, especially towards Tom, but Regina couldn't even begin to imagine what Joey and Jasper must have had to endure day after day.

181

"He is a good person," she said in a dying voice.

She felt powerless. She couldn't do anything to help her friend.

"He will be fine," Joey added softly.

"I hope." Regina shook her head. "I'm sorry, I'll pull myself together, I promise."

"You don't have to apologize," said Joey and made himself comfortable against the wall of the hut. "I have never known anyone who had such deep feelings for everything. It's actually great to see that there are people like that."

Regina's cheeks filled with blood. Joey seemed to like certain things about her she had never considered special herself and that others often saw as weakness.

"Are you an Andarian creature too?" she asked.

"Why?" Joey laughed.

"Because you see things others don't, and you help me see them as well."

Joey smiled.

"I hope that's a good thing."

"It's a good thing," said Regina, her voice a bit uneven. "Thanks."

They looked at the millions of stars sparking like tiny diamonds on the pitch black canvas that was the Andarian sky in comfortable silence. Regina let her head rest against the wall of the hut, and the magical peacefulness completely calmed her mind. She didn't even feel her eyelids closing as she drifted off to sleep.

13: AN UNFAMILIAR ACQUAINTANCE

When Regina woke up, she was in Joey's hut, tucked in bed. Joey was sleeping in the farthest corner, on the wooden floor, using a hoodie as a blanket and a pair of jeans as a pillow.

Regina smiled at the thought that she was so exhausted last night that she didn't even wake up when Joey carried her to bed.

The sun was up once again, and its rays shone through the old windows of the hut. Regina lay between the cozy white sheets for a while. She was looking at Joey's back, which was peeping out from beneath the hoodie he was using as a blanket. Regina found him adorably vulnerable as he was curled up on the floor, facing the wall. His hair was rumpled, and some of the black locks were scattered around the pair of jeans he rested his head on. Regina felt lucky she could share her Andarian journey with someone as nice as Joey.

She sat up on the bed quietly, carefully trying to make as little noise as possible, but Joey immediately started moving.

He scratched his head and turned over on the floor to face Regina. His brown eyes were still small as he looked at her.

"Good morning," he said in a raspy morning voice.

"Good morning," said Regina, smiling. "Thanks for bringing me in last night."

"You're welcome," replied Joey, and he turned on his back to rub his eyes.

"Wasn't it really uncomfortable down there?"

"It wasn't the most comfortable," answered Joey with a laugh.

Regina looked at the bed she was sitting on—it was easily big enough for two people. Joey sat up on the wooden floor with a painful grumble, and as he put his hand on his spine, Regina smiled.

"You're a good guy," she said.

"Hm?" Joey looked at her confused. "What do you mean?"

"I mean you're a good guy," repeated Regina as she got up from the bed and walked to the little kitchen area next to Joey.

"I'm going to make you breakfast to show you my gratitude," she said and began rummaging inside the kitchen cupboards.

"You really don't have to, but thank you," said Joey and sat on one of the old wooden chairs next to the little dining table.

Regina pulled out a jar of Nangrass from one of the cupboards. The tiny baby-looking plant was peacefully sleeping behind the glass. Regina carefully pulled out the skin it had shed off and put it into two mugs. She boiled some water in a cauldron and poured it in the mugs, then she slid one in front of Joey and took a sip from the other.

While Joey was sipping his tea, Regina put some fruits she found in the cupboards on a plate, in an appetizing display and sprinkled some kind of herbs on them, then she put the plate in the middle of the table. It tasted surprisingly good, and Regina started so suspect that it was not possible to make a foul-tasting dish from Andarian ingredients. By the time they finished eating, they were both completely awake, so they decided to go outside for a walk and look around.

"Do you remember where Dragon's Valley is? Did Agnitio take you there?" Regina asked when they stepped outside.

"I remember, yeah. Do you want to go? Maybe Brunorth is there?"

Regina nodded with excitement.

"It's good that you remember, because my sense of locality is horrible," she said as they set off.

Regina noticed something in the corner of her eye immediately as they left the hut—the horizon was not only one color anymore. There was a patch of darkness in the light blue starry horizon somewhere in the distance, beyond the sea—Mount Napharata. Also, on the left side of the horizon, the towers of Astraea's castle glistened between the stars if one looked closely enough to see.

"Were these visible before?" Regina asked.

"What do you mean?"

Regina stepped aside so Joey could see the horizon on their right.

"Wow," Joey said with surprise. "They were definitely not there. At least I didn't see them before. You didn't either?"

"No," replied Regina as they stopped to look at the divided horizon.

As Regina was looking at the dark smudge that was Mount Napharata, she felt angry. How did they have the nerve to do what they were doing? Why did a place like that even have to exist? Everything would have been so much better without them.

"Are you okay?" asked Joey, probably because Regina hadn't said anything for a while, and her facial expressions were always easy to read.

"I'm fine, I'm fine," she said, turning her head away from the horizon. "Let's just go."

They walked next to each other in silence. The sun was comfortably warm, and there was no one on the open field where there were no more huts.

After a good ten minutes of walking, a hut appeared on the field.

"That's Agnitio's, right?" asked Regina, and the childlike smile returned to her face once again.

"Yep," answered Joey with a smile.

Regina's face lit up, and she started running towards the hut, leaving Joey behind.

"That quirky faun is great to be around, huh?" said Joey

when he caught up to Regina, who was already standing in front of the wooden door of the hut.

"He's not home. Look." She pointed at the wooden sign on the door, which had the following carved into it: *Feel free to help yourself to some tea.*

"That's nice of him. Do you want to go in?"

"No, we just had tea," said Regina. "I hope we'll see him soon though. He is great to be around, isn't he?"

"Yeah, he has a good vibe for sure. I'm sure we'll see him soon."

Joey's sentence was followed by an angry grunt coming from the right side of the hut. Regina and Joey tilted their heads to see who had made the sound, and they saw a short elf, just like the one in Dara Forest, angrily working on something next to Agnitio's hut, in the grass.

The small elf kept grunting until he noticed Regina and Joey watching him, and then he looked at them with eyes wide open for a second, then burst out yelling: "You humans, I'm so sick of all of you!" His voice was high and crackling. "You come here and you think that you can just walk around this sacred land as you please! You don't even notice all the beauty you destroy! Like all the flowers that give their fragrance even to your foul feet that crush them!"

"I'm sorry, we didn't—" Regina tried to explain herself, but the small elf turned his hunched back on her before she could finish.

He took a potion bottle out of the huge utility belt around his waist and poured a couple of drops of its contents on something in front of him, then he angrily began waddling away, leaving a beautiful yellow flower behind.

"Did we step on that flower?" Regina asked quietly.

"No, we haven't even been there," said Joey. "These little creatures really hate us though." He crouched down to take a closer look at the yellow flower.

"Don't you dare pick it!" the small elf yelled at Joey from the distance.

"No, I was just—" Joey tried to explain himself, but the elf turned his back on them again and continued waddling away.

Regina laughed at the scene with her lips pushed together.

"Okay, I'll leave the flower alone then," said Joey and stood up from the ground.

"They're so funny, I can't handle it." Regina was having a hard time holding back her laughter.

The small elf disappeared in the distance, and Regina and Joey continued their walk towards Dragon's Valley.

As they were climbing the hill next to Agnitio's hut, Regina's heart kept beating faster and faster. Would Brunorth be there? Would they reunite? Or would Saphira not let him near her again? When they reached the top of the hill, Regina was only hoping to see the tiny dragon again, even from a distance.

She looked over Dragon's Valley with a tight stomach. The large green dragon was there, lying in the grass just like the first time Regina had been there. The brown dragon was standing and seemed to be eating grass. There was also a red one in the valley, who Regina hadn't seen last time.

Regina's eyes hopped from one dragon to another, eagerly searching for the color black, and somewhere in the distance, her eyes did find a large black spot.

As she adjusted her eyes to see more detail, she realized that the large black dragon was Saphira, and she was curled around a smaller black ball.

"He's being reborn." Regina got emotional.

"Is Brunorth that small black ball?" asked Joey. "Agnitio told me about the dragons' ability to be reborn, but none of them were in cocoons when I was here."

"Yes, I think Brunorth is that little ball," said Regina,

189

smiling. "Saphira formed a cocoon right in front of us when I was here. She was much smaller then. I wonder how Brunorth will turn out."

As Regina was looking at the tiny black ball that was Brunorth, all her dislike towards Saphira disappeared. She understood why she had taken Brunorth back. The peaceful moment, however, was interrupted by a familiar voice.

"Regina, hey!" shouted the voice, and in the next moment, Snow smashed into Regina from the side.

"Snow, hi!" said Regina and hugged Snow back.

She felt incredibly glad to see Snow. She didn't stay in Mount Napharata, she had made it back.

"I'm so glad you're back," Regina said emotionally.

"Of course I'm back," said Snow, pulling away from Regina to look at her face. "Why wouldn't I be?"

"You could have stayed in Mount Napharata. You were there, right?"

"Sure, Mount Napharata." Snow nodded. "I just don't get why anyone would stay there. That Red Queen was really creepy."

"Jasper stayed . . ." whispered Regina, looking at the ground.

"Oh . . ." Snow was surprised. "I'm so sorry."

Regina shook her head and looked at Snow with a forced smile.

"It's not your fault," she said then looked behind Snow and saw Pyro standing there.

"Hi, Regina." Pyro greeted her with an awkward wave.

"Hi." Regina was not glad to see Pyro Marblestone. She swallowed then asked Pyro, "So, you didn't stay in Mount Napharata either?" The question felt bitter in her mouth.

"No, as you can see." Pyro looked embarrassed, almost ashamed. "I'm right here."

"Yes, I can see that," said Regina with anger and turned her back on them, starting to walk away.

Joey must have remembered Snow and Pyro from Dara Forest, because he didn't say anything to them, he just stood there, looking uncomfortable in the situation.

Regina walked away from Snow. She felt like she couldn't contain her anger towards Pyro otherwise. All the sadness she felt about Jasper staying in Mount Napharata turned into anger towards Pyro in that moment. He was the one responsible for Jasper's hardships after all. He was the reason Jasper chose to stay in Mount Napharata.

"I'm so sorry." Regina heard Pyro's voice. It was weak, like a sick little boy's.

She turned around. The boy she saw standing in front of her was not familiar to her—Pyro stood there with his hands clasped in front of him, looking at the ground with shame written all over his face. Small tears appeared to sparkle under the blond locks that were covering his face.

Regina didn't know how to react to the broken boy who was standing in front of her. She didn't recognize this person—he was a stranger to her in that moment.

"I . . ." Pyro struggled to speak. "I really am so sorry. This place . . . it made me realize what I've done. I'm not

191

that person. I didn't even realize how I was behaving . . . I would like to apologize to Jasper if he'll hear me out."

Regina didn't know what to think of what she was hearing, but the rage that she felt didn't seem to subside with the boy's words. A dragon's roar shook the air here and there, but Regina was too furious to pay attention.

"Well, you can't do that now, can you?" she said, drops of anger spilling from her voice. "Jasper's in Mount Napharata because of you!"

Pyro bit his lips and looked down at the ground again. Snow stepped next to him and gently put her hand on his back. Regina shook her head and continued walking away.

"No, please!" Pyro shouted. "You need to hear me out!"

"Why?" Regina turned around with momentum that would have even made a lion freeze.

"Because I don't know how I'll be able to live with myself otherwise," answered Pyro.

Regina, once again, didn't know how to the react to the emotions that were swirling around inside of her. Pyro had made Jasper's life miserable, but the torn kid that was standing in front of her somehow didn't coincide with her memories.

"What do you need to tell me anyway?" Regina asked. "You don't even know me."

"You're right." Pyro gave up and waved his hand with defeat. "Forget it."

"No!" Snow joined in. "Regina, please, just listen to him!"

Regina rolled her eyes. She didn't have anything else to

add to the drama.

"Okay, whatever." Regina gave in. "Things can't get any worse anyways." She sat down on the ground and looked at Pyro with impatient eyes. "Please, take a seat and elaborate." Regina pointed at the ground in front of her, her voice filled with as much sarcasm as she could squeeze out from herself.

Pyro sat down on the ground, keeping his distance from Regina. Even his movements seemed pitiable now. Snow stayed on her feet next to Pyro, and Joey did the same behind Regina.

"So," Pyro began quietly as he played with the grass in front of him.

"I can't hear you! No point in blabbing if I can't even hear!" Regina let every ounce of her anger flow into her voice.

"So," Pyro started again, this time louder, enduring Regina's rage like a well-deserved punishment. "I don't even know why I want to tell you this . . ."

"That's great then," said Regina.

"But," continued Pyro, "I still feel that I need to tell you for some reason."

Regina didn't say anything. She hated to admit it, but how Pyro was talking felt sincere. Even though he was the same Pyro on the outside—the Pyro that Regina often thought of as pure evil—Regina couldn't deny him the opportunity to share his apology. She hated Pyro for all that he had done, but somehow the pity she felt for the broken boy sitting in front of her slowly started to overpower her anger.

"This whole journey here in Andara really changed me," said Pyro. "I didn't realize who I became in the process of trying to save myself. I was so afraid that I didn't see anything beyond myself, you know?"

"No, I don't know." Regina was starting to lose her patience.

"Ah," sighed Pyro, uncomfortably scratching his head.

"You can tell her, Pyro," said Snow in a gentle voice, but Pyro didn't say anything.

"Okay, thank you," said Regina and began getting up from the ground.

"I was just like Jasper once." Pyro spat the words out like they were hot coals in his mouth.

Regina dropped back onto the ground. She couldn't say anything.

Pyro started breathing rapidly and said, "Before I came to this school, I was bullied. Three large guys used to beat me up every single day. I couldn't tell my parents, because my dad is a typical tough guy, and he would have probably disowned me or something. When I came to this school, I was scared to death that it would happen again. I made friends with the biggest and loudest guy I could find, and I hoped that would prevent me from becoming a victim again. I wanted to avoid being the target so bad, I didn't even notice that I became the bully myself. I just wanted you to know that I see now, and I won't hurt anyone from now on." Pyro didn't look at Regina, his fingers kept flicking the grass in front of him. His eyes weren't filled with tears, and there was no self-pity in his voice as he spoke.

"I see." Regina's voice was quiet. She felt the huge blame she had put on Pyro slowly slip away, leaving only empty desperation behind. "I'm sorry."

Pyro looked at her. When their eyes met, he shook his head and looked back at the ground again.

"No, please," he said. "Don't feel sorry."

Regina took a deep breath.

"I understand then," she said. "How come you only realized it now?"

"The Mirror of Saccai . . ." Pyro's voice was so quiet, Regina almost couldn't hear him.

"You reached the Island of Pyara too?" Regina narrowed her eyes.

Pyro nodded.

Regina couldn't process this information immediately. Wasn't the Island of Pyara supposed to be a place only a few reached? If it was, that meant Regina had been wrong about Pyro. As she looked at the embarrassed boy playing with the grass, she felt like she didn't know who he truly was. All the labels she had put on him throughout the years—evil, monster—they all seemed to lose their meaning.

"I'm not the one who should be forgiving you," she said.

"I know," replied the boy. "I want to go back to Mount Napharata and talk to him."

"You should," agreed Regina. This conversation felt surreal to her. "Where's Clive, by the way?"

"He went home right after the incident in Dara Forest,"

said Pyro.

"What was that anyway?" asked Snow with a smile.

"It was really cool." Pyro's eyes looked like he hadn't slept in weeks. He looked up at Joey, who was still standing a little further away.

"Well, that's a pretty long story," answered Joey and stepped next to Regina.

"We have time," said Snow and sat next to Pyro.

Joey looked at Regina, checking if she wanted this conversation to continue. Regina shrugged, so Joey sat down next to her.

"Well, I'm a Nayaka." Joey went on to explain what he had learned about being a Nayaka with openness surprising from him.

"Wow, that's amazing," said Snow when Joey finished the explanation.

"You're someone to look up to then, basically," said Pyro. "I didn't even introduce myself yet. I'm Pyro Mablestone." Pyro reached towards Joey with his right hand.

"Joey Herd." Joey shook his hand.

"And I'm Snow Gamy." Snow reached towards Joey as well, and Joey shook hands with her too.

"Where are you from, Joey?" asked Snow.

"I'm from the fifth district of Tupsbade."

"Oh, cool, that's not far at all then," said Snow.

It still felt weird to Regina that the four of them were sitting on a hill together, peacefully talking. She kept looking at Pyro with suspicious eyes. He seemed exhausted. He probably wasn't comfortable in the situation either, because he didn't really contribute to the conversation. Joey and Snow kept the talk flowing for a while.

"Right, Regina?"

Regina looked at Snow at the mention of her name.

"Hmm?"

"I just told Joey that we've known each other since forever."

"Oh, yeah, forever." Regina nodded.

"That's great," said Joey. "I never really had a good friend," he added, embarrassedly scratching his head.

"I know what you mean," said Pyro, looking up at Joey with eyes that seemed even more tired than a couple of minutes ago.

"Hey!" Snow playfully pushed Pyro's shoulder. "I'm your good friend!"

"Yeah, since like a month ago." A smile lit up Pyro's fatigued face. "I meant before you."

"But I'm a good friend, right?" asked Snow, trying to make Pyro smile for a little longer.

"You know you are, Whitey," replied Pyro, and he also playfully pushed Snow's shoulder.

Regina became even more confused as she watched them. *Whitey?* They seemed to be really good friends, and Pyro appeared to genuinely care for Snow. The blond boy sitting in front of her became more and more unfamiliar by the minute.

"Snow helped me a lot actually," said Pyro. "Without her,

I would probably still be a jerk. She was the first person I could honestly talk to. She didn't judge me."

Regina's chest suddenly tightened as her own experience with Joey came to her mind. She refused to judge Joey too based on the seemingly horrible things he had done, because she knew somehow that Joey must have had a good reason. Was Pyro no different? Was she just too involved in the situation to see?

"I know what you mean," said Joey.

Regina looked at him for a moment then averted her eyes with an embarrassed smile.

Regina started to realize that Pyro was probably not the horrible person she had thought he was, and she couldn't help but smile at the duo in front of her. In that moment, she felt that everything might turn out well after all.

"Fraternizing with the enemy, I see," said a voice Regina immediately recognized. Jasper was walking up the hill, towards them.

"Jas—" Regina saw what Jasper was carrying in his left hand. Her burst of joy quickly faded, and terror took its place.

14. A PROMISE KEPT

Regina recognized what Jasper was carrying in his hand, and she immediately knew why he was there. The brown teddy bear wearing glasses and a lab coat used to be with Jasper all the time. It hung from his backpack until the fourth grade, when Pyro transferred to the school. It was the first thing he teased Jasper with.

The bear looked old and ragged as it hung from the approaching Jasper's hand. Regina's eyes noticed something immediately on the bear's white coat; it looked like something had been burned into the fabric, but Regina couldn't manage to read what.

"So, what's up here?" asked Jasper with forced poise when he arrived next to them.

"What's up with you?" asked Regina, and she stood up from the ground to hug Jasper, but the boy pushed her away.

"I don't mingle with traitors," he said.

"Traitors? Jasper, what are you talking about?"

"I've been gone for two seconds, and you have already

signed the peace treaty with this lesser human? Is he your new best friend now?" Jasper didn't leave time for Regina to react, he turned towards Joey with resentment. "Joey, man, really? The Nayaka too? Humanity really is hopeless, I guess."

Joey opened his mouth to react, but Pyro was faster; he stood up and said, "Jasper . . . I'm glad you're here. I was about to go to Mount Napharata to talk to you."

Jasper looked at Pyro with a hint of nervousness in his eyes; he didn't react to his words immediately.

"I didn't come to talk," Jasper said finally and threw the bear in front of Pyro.

What was burned into the bear's white coat became undeniably visible as it unfolded on the grass for all of them to see; the words *TIME FOR REVENGE* tainted the once spotless coat.

When Regina saw the words, one thing came to her mind immediately: Eris. This must have been his attempt to push Jasper over the line, just like he had promised.

Regina stepped in front of Jasper, shaking her head in fear, and Joey and Snow stood up from the ground as well.

"Please, Jasper," whispered Regina. "I just talked to him. Just hear him out. You don't have to do this. Don't let them push you over the line."

Jasper looked into Regina's eyes like she was someone despicable and said, "I have no choice. I'm tired of being the victim."

When he finished the sentence, a black cloud of smoke

appeared next to him. Regina stepped back, and a figure emerged from the smoke—it was the Red Queen. She put her arms around Jasper with a smug smile on her face.

"Jasper, dear, I'm so proud of you," she said in her deep but whiny voice. "This is how you take charge of your destiny! Something these trash know nothing about!"

She looked at Regina, Joey, Snow and Pyro with disgust. The behavior of the red-haired woman had completely changed towards them since the last time they had seen her. The forcibly nice woman who wanted to worm herself into their trust was no more. The contempt she was feeling towards them was unambiguous and apparent.

"Those who reject Lord Ate don't deserve to live!" she yelled, and a hint of madness appeared in her eyes for a moment.

Regina and Joey both stepped back next to Snow and Pyro. They watched the Red Queen and Jasper, but neither of them could say anything.

"See?" The Red Queen pointed at them and looked at Jasper. "See how afraid they are of you? Doesn't it feel great?"

A small smile appeared on Jasper's face, and it broke Regina's heart. She helplessly shook her head and felt her eyes fill up with tears. *How did it come to this?*

The Red Queen opened her right palm in front of herself, and as she smiled smugly at them, black smoke appeared above her palm, and a dagger fell into her hand. Its grip was black with gold detail, and the blade shone with a gray coating.

"This is the Dagger of Badala," she said, holding the dagger in front of Jasper. "It only appears before the truly worthy. You, Jasper, are one of the most honorable people I have ever had the pleasure of knowing."

Jasper looked at the blade for a moment then took it from the Red Queen. He had a look in his eyes Regina had not seen before. He seemed overwhelmed, but still hauntingly empty. The boy standing in front of Regina was just as unfamiliar to her as Pyro was not so long ago, but this was not a pleasant disappointment—it was a heartbreakingly horrible one.

"Woah," said Pyro and took a step back, "that's a little extreme, isn't it?"

"Extreme?" asked the Red Queen with a contorted face. "What's the appropriate punishment for victimizing someone in your eyes, Blondie?"

Pyro couldn't answer, he just shook his head, desperately protesting the situation. Snow stepped closer to him, and her stance told that she was prepared to jump in front of Pyro if it was needed.

"Jasper," said Joey, taking a step towards Jasper, "you're not serious, are you? This is not who you want to be, dude."

"What do you know?" whispered Jasper with both anger and sadness in his voice. "I'm not a perfect Nayaka like you. Certain things have to be done if one wants to move forward!"

The Dagger of Badala started to glow with a red light as

202

Jasper was talking.

"That's right," said the Red Queen, smiling. "The Dagger of Badala senses your power, Jasper. The more you want to use it, the more power it will give you. This here . . . this red glow . . . it's the sign of true power. You are so amazing, Jasper."

"Jasper, you can't do this!" Regina broke out in tears and jumped in front of Jasper to hug him, but Jasper angrily pushed her away, and Regina fell on the ground.

"No!" she yelled, immediately standing up. "I won't let you do this! Snap out of it! Just listen to what Pyro has to say!" she shouted in Jasper's face.

Jasper raised his hand and slapped Regina in the face with full force. Regina fell on the ground again, but this time she didn't get back up.

A heavy flow of tears started flowing down her face, which she buried into the grass. Snow squealed and crouched down next to her.

"Who do you think you are, telling me what to do? You lost your right to speak to me when you befriended this trash!"

"How dare you hit her?" Joey's voice crackled in an unusual way.

Regina turned her head just enough to see Joey. The boy was looking at the ground, and his hands were fisted at his sides, almost shaking.

"How dare you . . . ?" Joey whispered with fury as he looked up at Jasper.

Regina could see, even from the ground, that Joey's eyes had lost their warm brown color—they were empty and white.

"You can't quite control yourself yet, can you, Nayaka?" said the Red Queen cockily. "You know, it would be much easier if you would just let it take you. It's not your fault for being like this. It's everybody else's fault for not accepting you the way you are. We would accept you at Mount Napharata, you know. No one knows what you're going through more than I do."

Regina sat up and looked at Joey with concern. The boy appeared to be struggling with his feelings as he stared in front of himself with blank white eyes. Jasper took two steps back from him and kept glancing at the Red Queen, probably in hopes of some assistance.

"No . . ." Joey stuttered. "I will not . . . choose"—he took a deep breath and closed his eyes for a couple of seconds; when he opened them again, the brown color was warmer in them than ever—"the easy way out." He finished his sentence in a confident voice.

The Red Queen snorted indifferently.

"Don't come crying to me when your little friends abandon you. No one stands by a Nayaka for long, kid. We're too special," she said, and Regina noticed an all too human hurt in her eyes.

"Who I am doesn't depend on others," said Joey and stepped back in front of Pyro.

Regina and Snow got up from the ground as well and

stood next to Joey, making their defensive wall in front of Pyro wider.

"Thanks, guys," Pyro whispered. He didn't seem to think he deserved their protection.

Regina wiped the tears off her face, and when she looked at her hands, she noticed they were bloody. Jasper had hit her hard. Regina felt her stomach clutch. Her heart beating violently against her chest could have made her panic easily, but she wiped her hands on her pants, took a deep breath and straightened her back. She didn't want to choose the easy way out either.

"We will not let you hurt him, Jasper," she said in a shaking, but still determined voice. "You might not want to listen to him, you might not want to accept his apology, but that does not mean you can do whatever you want, and it certainly does not mean that you're right."

Jasper shook his head with disappointment as he looked at Regina.

"You really are a she-devil," he said.

The Red Queen laughed out loud at his insult, which made Jasper smile. Regina's chest tightened, but she didn't let herself show any sort of reaction.

"You don't know anything, just get out of the way!" Jasper shouted, and the red glow around the dagger grew even bigger.

"That's right, Jasper!" said the Red Queen. "That's your power, right there! Show them you are not the victim anymore! Be the hero!"

Jasper started breathing heavily, and as he was looking at the blade, the red glow grew stronger.

Regina turned her head to look at Pyro and whispered, "Wish yourself back home."

"I tried. I can't." Pyro's eyes were flooded with fear.

"Then run," Snow whispered.

Pyro carefully took a few steps back and then tried to run down the hill, but before his foot could even touch the ground, the Red Queen raised her left hand towards him, and Pyro froze mid-movement, helplessly falling down to the ground.

"Blondie!" yelled the Red Queen, laughing. "How pathetic you are! The tables have turned!"

Regina tried to turn around to help Pyro, but the Red Queen raised her right hand towards them, and Regina couldn't move anymore. She felt all her strength leave her limbs, and fell to the ground. Joey and Snow seemed to be experiencing the same—they both fell down next to Regina.

Regina could swear the sky looked darker than before. The bright blue Andarian sky seemed to be dulled by a gray layer of smoke—everything suddenly seemed so dim and colorless, and even the silence of the air was filled with a fizzling noise.

"Well, well, well . . ." said the Red Queen nonchalantly as she walked between them. The bottom of her black silk dress rolled on the grass like drops of mercury, rejected by the earth. "Are you starting to regret your choices now? It certainly feels like you're on the wrong side now, doesn't it?

206

Some people are just so pitiful."

"You're . . . the one . . . who's pitiful . . ." Joey forced the words out of his helpless body.

Regina's heart was beating madly in the vulnerable situation, but she gathered all of her strength and moved her head slightly in order to see what was going on.

The Red Queen crouched down next to the paralyzed Joey. The expression on her face didn't hide the outrage she was feeling.

"Let's see which one of us is pitiful, Nayaka," she said, and with her sharp red nails, she drew an invisible sign in the air, in front of Joey.

Joey's powerless body couldn't express the pain he was feeling properly, only a painfully weak moan left his mouth as his body shook with torment.

The Red Queen stood up and slid back next to Jasper, leaving the shaking Joey behind.

Tears poured from Regina's eyes as she had to watch her friend in such pain. She tried with all her strength to get up, but she only managed to make her limbs shake excessively. Joey's body started to calm down after a little while, and he shakily turned his head towards Regina and smiled at her to let her know that he was fine. Regina managed to move her facial muscles and somewhat smile back at the boy.

"Jasper, do you think we're the pitiful ones?" asked the Red Queen.

Regina gathered her strength and moved her head to look at Jasper. The Dagger of Badala was glowing brighter than ever in his hands. As Regina was watching them, even the sounds she was hearing seemed muffled.

Jasper was staring in the direction where Pyro had fallen. He began moving his legs towards him. He dragged his feet across the grass like a tiger approaching his pray.

Regina gathered all her strength again to move her head and saw that Jasper had stopped in front of Pyro. He kept looking at the paralyzed boy, who was defenselessly lying before him.

Pyro moved his eyes to the very side in order to look at Jasper. Tears were dripping from his face as he looked at the boy he had been terrorizing for so long.

Regina was trying to move or speak and somehow get Jasper to snap out of the mindset he was in, but the invisible force holding her down was too strong, and the Jasper she knew seemed to be far away in that moment.

"Do it, Jasper!" said the Red Queen. "It's the only way you can redeem your pride!"

The sky turned even darker as the black mist seemed to fill up the air around them.

Regina didn't take her eyes off Jasper and Pyro. She was still hoping that somehow she would be able to say or do something in the last moment that would prevent Jasper from acting. She still didn't fully believe that Jasper was capable of hurting Pyro. She couldn't let herself believe that.

Regina saw Jasper lifting up the dagger above Pyro, and she desperately tried to move, only causing her whole body to shake. *No . . . This can't actually happen . . .*

"Don't let anger take away the choices you have yet to make, Jasper." A familiar voice rang softly across the dark air.

Regina recognized Astraea's voice. She didn't show herself, at least Regina didn't see her, but her gentle sound embraced to colorless scene.

"I know you can hear me," Astraea continued. "I've been with you when you were just a child. Do you remember how we used to play? How much we used to laugh? I know you remember. Allow yourself to listen to me, please Jasper. Everything will be all right, I promise. Jasper . . . you are so much more than this."

Regina felt another flow of tears stream down her face as she was listening to Astraea's words. She kept her eyes on Jasper, who was still holding the dagger above the helpless Pyro, and she saw a white light surround Jasper in the dark air. This light dimmed the dark mist, and it dimmed the bright red glow of the dagger as well. As Regina was looking at this soft white light, she saw the vague shape of Astraea in it, holding Jasper in a tight embrace.

The sight of Astraea's glowing figure protecting Jasper made Regina feel like hope was still not lost. Jasper still didn't strike with the dagger, he still had the chance to turn back. Regina kept repeating the message she wanted to send Jasper in her mind. *Put the dagger down, Jasper. Just put it down, put it down . . . Please, Jasper . . .*

None of them could do anything. Regina, Snow and Joey were paralyzed on the ground, just like Pyro. The Red

Queen was cheering Jasper on, and Astraea tried her best to get to a boy who had lost the ability to see her long ago. Everyone present wanted Jasper to act one way or another, but none of them had real say in what was about to happen—it all came down to Jasper.

He stood still, with his hands above Pyro. He didn't put the dagger down, but he didn't swing it towards Pyro either. When Regina felt like she couldn't take it anymore, a deep roar tore across the misty air. A moment later, a black creature flew in front of Jasper, blowing another loud roar in his face.

Jasper fell back, dropping the Dagger of Badala, which

immediately disappeared before even reaching the ground. Astraea's white glow was nowhere to be seen anymore either.

As Regina focused her eyes on the four-legged creature, she recognized the eyes of the black dragon—it was Brunorth. He was much larger than before, but Regina couldn't make out any more differences in that moment.

Jasper crawled back to the Red Queen in a panic.

"Foul creature!" the Red Queen shouted at Brunorth. "You should have stayed in your disgusting cocoon, you useless lizard!"

Brunorth growled at the Red Queen, still standing in front of Pyro.

Regina could still only manage to make her body shake in desperation when she tried to gather her strength to move her limbs, and what she saw of Pyro, Snow and Joey, they were experiencing the same thing. The Red Queen turned her back on them and looked down onto the Field of Cetana, and Jasper turned towards the field as well.

"Desperate hearts of all who reside on the Field of Cetana, hear my call!" shouted the Red Queen in a voice that echoed through the air. "The one true leader, Lord Ate, awaits your arrival at Mount Napharata! Together, we will make the most of your potential, and guide you towards greatness!"

"Stand up, friends," a familiarly calm voice broke through the noise, and the bottom of a worn brown robe entered Regina's field of vision.

211

"Stand up," Agnitio repeated. His voice didn't sound worried at all.

Regina tried as hard as she could to move, but it didn't get any easier. How could they just stand up? Wasn't that supposed to be impossible?

"Turn your fear around," said Agnitio. "The other side of it is strength."

Regina didn't realize how afraid she was until then, but she suddenly grew conscious of the heavy weight of fear inside her body. Still, she was just Regina. Agnitio might have managed to stand up, but how could she?

"Strength lies somewhere deep inside of fear," said Agnitio. "Search for it."

It was worth at least a try. Regina closed her eyes and concentrated her attention on the fear she was feeling. The uncomfortable knot in her stomach, the tingling in her hands—yes, she was deathly afraid. What happened then truly surprised Regina: the moment she saw what she was feeling from the outside, she felt an enormous sense of power. Why should she surrender to this feeling? Yes, it was there, but who cares? *It's just a feeling.*

She tried to move her arms again, and this time they obeyed her. She got up from the ground, placing her feet next to each other thoughtfully. As she straightened up, she saw Agnitio standing next to them with his hands gently placed behind his back and a joyful expression on his face. In the dramatically dark situation, the cheerful faun looked incongruous.

212

Regina smiled at him with gratitude then turned around and saw that Snow, Joey and Pyro were up on their feet as well. All of them looked disheveled but not broken.

"What is the meaning of this?" yelled the Red Queen when she turned around and saw them. "How did you manage to . . . ? Agnitio!"

"Bellator," Agnitio greeted her with a polite nod.

The Red Queen's expression turned furious as she pressed her lips together and snorted like an angry bull.

"It doesn't matter," she said with a smirk. "Humans will keep on joining us at Mount Napharata, and you know you can't do anything about it."

Agnitio's expression lacked all signs of concern as he stood peacefully, slightly smiling at the Red Queen. Regina was amazed by how calm he managed to stay in every situation. It seemed like nothing could come between the faun and his peace.

"You underestimate humans, Bellator," he said. "By the way, you're always welcome back here if you ever decide to change your mind."

Regina's and Jasper's eyes met through the mist, and Regina saw the face of a boy who was looking for liberation in all the wrong places. She still wanted to hug him and tell him that the answer was simpler than he thought, but she knew that it wouldn't change anything.

The Red Queen looked at Agnitio with fury, and in the next moment Jasper and she were gone, leaving only a black cloud and the ragged teddy bear behind. The dark layer of mist that hid the color of the land disappeared with them, and the peaceful silence returned once again.

The tall faun walked to the lonely stuffed animal and lifted it up from the ground.

"Oh, Jasper . . ." Agnitio sighed. He then looked at Regina. "It's nice to see you all again." He was smiling, but his eyes revealed the hurt he was feeling.

The moment felt bittersweet to Regina. They were all alive; Jasper didn't put down the Dagger of Badala, but he didn't strike with it in the end either. Regina felt like she could fall apart any moment, but the calm aura of Agnitio somehow made her feel like there was no need to worry. Brunorth waddled next to her, and she hugged him.

"Thank you again, little friend," she whispered. "You're not so little anymore though, are you?"

The dragon was about as big as a large dog, and his head and body seemed more muscular than before. His features became longer and sharper, just like the spikes on his back and wings.

"Brunorth did a great job with his rebirth," said Agnitio, walking back to them. "It is very clear that you influenced his new form, Regina."

"I did?" asked Regina in a dying voice.

"Yes," said Agnitio, nodding. "His transformation came from his heart. It will make him one of the strongest dragons one day."

Regina looked at Brunorth with a tired but proud smile. Joey, Snow and Pyro all gathered around him.

"Did he only get bigger?" Joey asked, crouching down next to the dragon and petting his head.

It seemed like no one could or wanted to speak about what had happened.

"The most important transformation dragons go through during rebirth is not on the outside," Agnitio explained.

The dragon didn't seem to mind the presence of people like he did before. He comfortably stood between all of them, serving as diversion from the events that had taken place.

"Thank you so much, Brunorth," whispered Pyro as he also crouched down next to the dragon.

Regina and Joey stood up to give the blond boy time with the one who had possibly saved his life. Brunorth looked at him and softly grunted.

"Why couldn't I go back home, Agnitio?" asked Pyro like he was too tired to care about the answer.

"There are certain moments you can't escape from. Not even in Andara," said Agnitio.

Pyro looked anguished, but the clear look in his eyes told Regina he was going to be okay. Maybe not that day or the next, but someday.

Snow stood collected, but the deep breaths she was often taking revealed that she, too, was shook up. Joey didn't show any sign of weakness or despair as he looked at Brunorth with his arms folded before him. Regina herself felt tired and overwhelmed, but she tried to keep herself as calm as she could.

She rested her eyes on Agnitio; looking at the faun somehow kept her from falling apart. Agnitio kept examining the ragged teddy bear with his eyes, which were not as peaceful as usual—they were tinted with sorrow, but when Agnitio looked up at Regina, he smiled, and the joyful sparkle returned to them. Regina smiled back at him, but as she curved her mouth, the weight of all that had happened flushed her eyes with tears. There was nothing to say.

15: CHOICES ONCE MADE

Despite everything that had happened, Regina, Joey, Snow and Pyro didn't show any willingness towards leaving Andara. They stood quietly on the hilltop for a while, directing their eyes at either Brunorth, Dragon's Valley or the Field of Cetana. The silence was heavy with the weight of the experience they had all shared. This invisible bond tied them together—leaving Andara now would have meant running away like a coward too afraid to face the reality in front of him. After all that had happened, they no longer had the comfort of leaving unknowingly. This silence was perhaps their respectful goodbye to the carefree ignorance they had lost.

The luxury of shutting down the TV when the daily news became too uncomfortable to watch was no longer an option. What Regina was most afraid of had somehow crawled into the heart of her best friend like a parasitic worm, and she found herself looking straight into the eyes of the darkness of man. She had to stay and stand its gaze, and so did Joey, Snow and Pyro, otherwise their unconcern would have given it the terrifying power of roaming free. As they stood in the heavy silence, they knew there was only one plague larger than the world's hostility—its indifference. And they didn't want to be a part of that plague.

"If you plant a flower," said Agnitio suddenly, "and it doesn't blossom, you don't blame the flower. You don't rip it out of the ground, throwing it away because it's faulty. You understand that it is probably lacking something essential for its bloom. Just because we don't know what to do with it, doesn't mean it cannot be helped. As long as you are alive, everything is possible." He then placed his hands behind his back, together with the ragged teddy bear, and began leisurely walking away.

Regina, Joey, Snow and Pyro looked at each other, confused by his words, but Regina mostly kept her eyes on the departing faun's back. With every step he took, the weight on Regina's chest became heavier and heavier until she finally forced a deep breath down her throat and ran after him. When she tugged on the elbow of his old brown robe, Agnitio stopped and looked back down at Regina, who was a little embarrassed by what she was doing.

"Can I . . . can I come with you?"

"Of course," said Agnitio.

"Thank you," whispered Regina and let go of Agnitio's robe.

She turned back to wave goodbye to the others, who waved back to her. It seemed like they understood each other without words. When Brunorth realized Regina was leaving, he ran after her, and they set off together.

The land didn't seem to gain back its color since the dark mist had descended upon it. The once lively green field now seemed dry to Regina. She kept looking at her feet sliding across the coarse grass, and tried to make sense of the fact that Andara didn't feel as peaceful to her as before. Just like the rough grass under her feet, the land itself had lost its color and softness. The magical land that seemed to be so far from reality, that even made time stop for a short while, somehow became more real and serious than Regina's life back home ever was. She kept looking at her feet, and soon enough, the only sound she could hear was the crackle of the thirsty grass against the rubber soles of her shoes. She became so submerged in the unpleasant sound she forced herself to listen to that she didn't notice Agnitio had stopped, so she bumped right into his back.

The smell that flew into her nose from the faun's old robe made her loosen her muscles in relaxation. The comforting smell of earth and flowers even made her shut her eyes for a brief moment again. Just like the first time they had met.

"Oh, I'm sorry," she said quickly, after realizing what she was doing, and took a step back from Agnitio.

Agnitio just smiled and invited her into his hut, which they had already reached without Regina realizing.

"Thank you," she said and walked into the hut with Brunorth.

"Make yourself at home," said Agnitio and walked to the

219

kitchen area.

Regina sat down at the table and Brunorth curled up under her chair. She rested her eyes on the faun, who was making something in the kitchen what Regina thought to be Nangrass tea. She felt like if she took her eyes off Agnitio, if she looked at the vicious world around her, it would have swallowed her whole.

Agnitio placed a white mug in front of Regina.

"Thank you," she said quietly.

She felt grateful to Agnitio for caring about her enough to make her tea in that moment when she felt so incredibly vulnerable.

She looked inside the mug in front of her. The tea was not crimson like last time—it was dark blue, almost black; it looked like a tiny, stormy sea.

"Wasn't Nangrass tea red last time?" she asked, doubting her own memory before anything else.

"It was," answered Agnitio. "However, it's not the tea that has changed. It's the drinker."

"So it is a different color," she said with tired realization. "But it's because of me, isn't it?"

Agnitio patiently nodded.

"Nangrass is an empathetic plant," he explained. "It adapts to its drinker's emotional state."

As Regina looked at the stormy waters of the dark liquid in front of her, she couldn't have agreed more with the representation it chose for her current mood.

"It's doing a good job," she said half-seriously.

Agnitio took a sip of his own tea, and Regina sneaked a peek at its color—she hadn't noticed last time that Agnitio's tea was as clear as water.

"That's not water, is it?" she asked, already suspecting the answer.

Agnitio softly shook his head.

"Yours never changes, does it?"

The faun shook his head again. Regina nodded and took a sip from her own tea. The warm liquid flowing through her felt like the comforting hug of an old friend, and it managed to lift Regina's spirits just a little bit.

"Thank you for letting me come with you. I hope I'm not too much of a bother."

"Seeing Andara is a painful experience," said Agnitio. "People often do anything in order to avoid it. The Island of Pyara is just as much of a part of this land as Mount Napharata. That's how it always was, and that's how it always will be. Facing the darkness will never be painless. But nothing can be overcome without looking it in the eye first."

Regina looked at the dark tea that sat between her nervously playing hands. Her eyes were sore, she was not sure why exactly, but she found herself blurting out the words, "Will Jasper overcome it?"

Agnitio looked at her in silence for a couple of seconds then said, "The voice Jasper chose to listen to is in your head as well. It's the same voice you chose to discard. Sometimes fear makes us think others are different from us,

221

but if we look deeply, we discover the same darkness in ourselves. We all have our own dark companions, even I. What determines a person is how they approach that companion."

Regina didn't take her eyes off the almost black liquid in front of her. Her eyes were half-closed from exhaustion.

"A man who has looked himself in the eye will never again be afraid of another," added Agnitio.

Everything had happened so fast after they arrived in Andara, Regina didn't even have time to think about the experiences she had had. Now that her tired eyes had the chance to rest on the strangely calming movements of the empathetic Nangrass tea, she could bring those memories out of the closet of her mind.

She remembered the comfortable feeling that surged over her in Mount Napharata. The feeling of being a person who was able to make her disinterested mother and absent father proud and happy. For a brief moment, when she was holding that shiny award, she felt like she was enough, like she was capable. And as she rested her eyes on the Nangrass tea now and thought back to that experience, it was like looking at a completely different person. She had changed so much almost overnight, and she didn't even realize it.

If she felt this much comfort, safety and hope in Mount Napharata, how much more must have Jasper felt? Regina had basically grown up with him, she saw how much the bullying hurt him, and how that hurt slowly transformed into growing anger inside of him. Looking back at everything Jasper had to live with, the conclusion he had come to didn't seem illogical to Regina at all. Wrong, for sure, but not at all illogical. Jasper's situation probably made it easy for the Napharatians to convince him to stay there. Regina sighed deeply at the realization.

"Those who cause suffering," said Agnitio, "they are suffering deeply themselves. It's important to remember that."

"And what can we do to change that?" asked Regina in a dying voice.

"Understand them," replied Agnitio. "Understanding doesn't leave room for anger, hurt or fear."

As Regina looked at Agnitio, she noticed that the faun had put Jasper's teddy bear on one of the shelves behind him.

"Why did you keep that, Agnitio?" she asked.

"Oh, the bear, yes," said Agnitio as he turned around in his chair to look at it. "Well, this old hut is full of knick-knacks as you can see. You might think something like this has never happened before, but these events are actually rather common here. Like that strange rock over there on the fourth shelf. A boy in 1943 tried to fashion a weapon in Mount Napharata to exterminate all of us here on the Field of Cetana. He gathered quite a few followers as well. That paper over there on the third shelf is a blueprint of the field a girl drew in 1892. There were some people here she considered her enemies. I remember the story of all these items like they happened today." Agnitio turned back towards Regina and joyfully smiled. "They keep reminding me of human nature."

Regina looked at all the items on the shelves. They all seemed old and unusable, some even unrecognizable, but Regina knew they all carried a memory. Each and every one of the strange items was a piece from Agnitio's infinite past, and they probably didn't, not for one second, allow the faun to have futile hope in humanity. The probable histories of the many objects on the shelves didn't help elevate Regina's mood one bit.

"That's horrible," she said.

"Do you think?" asked Agnitio.

"Well, isn't it?" asked Regina in confusion, not understanding how the tragic history of man could be anything but horrible.

Agnitio smiled.

"Do you see that dried up flower on the second shelf? A girl gave it to the boy who made the rock weapon. They were good friends who had chosen different paths. That flower, and of course what it stood for, made the boy realize he didn't want to harm the Cetanians. That plastic ball over there belonged to a boy who managed to bring the Napharatians and the Cetanians together for a peaceful bonfire in Dara Forest. That night created a bond so strong, it completely eliminated violence for years. For every item that carries the darkness of humanity there's one that holds the light. And that light is worth believing in."

Regina's eyes filled with tears as they glided through all

the different items in the old hut.

"Not just in others, but in yourself as well," added Agnitio.

When Regina felt the tears in her eyes were about to roll down her face, she turned her head back towards the cup of tea in front of her.

"I'll try . . . to believe," she mumbled.

Regina lifted her head to look at the items again. All the old, seemingly meaningless objects felt like they were alive somehow. As Regina looked at them, she started feeling less alone. So many of the people these objects once belonged to had had to face the same darkness she was facing right now. She wasn't the first one, and she won't be the last. In fact, probably many more people were facing the same back in the other world, right now. She was not alone.

She took a deep breath as she allowed the bonding force to enter her heart. This feeling of unity made her feel just a little stronger, like she was actually able to live through all that had happened and stand strongly on her feet. Through the objects on the shelves, many people were holding her hand after all.

As she looked at the items, she imagined their stories. They all had peaceful endings, because next to every tragic item, there was another that carried the power of change. She felt like the kind souls of the objects' owners were there smiling at her, inviting Regina to add her own item to their collection. Regina wondered what kind of object she would leave on these shelves. She wanted to add one, and she knew that something was still missing from Agnitio's hut—the item that could stand next to Jasper's teddy bear. When she finished looking at all of them, she looked at Agnitio and smiled.

"The Universe is friendly after all, isn't it?" Agnitio asked with a smile.

Regina's eyes filled with a fresh dose of tears, and she emotionally nodded. She looked at the objects again. The stories behind them were all choices once made. Who she would become in this situation was hers. Just like Joey chose to fight his own darkness, and Pyro put a stop to his. There was still light in the world, and the choice was hers to be a part of it.

"Thank you, Agnitio." Regina's voice was still weak, but now filled with new-found determination.

Agnitio smiled and nodded.

"You weren't just imagining the owners of all these items, you know," he said. "Every human who visits Andara leaves an imprint of their souls behind. This imprint forever stays here, holding the power of choices once made and determining the other world's balance."

Regina didn't say anything for a short while, she allowed Agnitio's words to sink in.

"That's . . ." she said, gathering her thoughts, "responsibility."

"Human life carries a great responsibility, yes," said Agnitio. "Man's irony is that the human mind often fails to recognize this responsibility. Dangerous ruler, the human mind. Marvelous servant, but dangerous ruler."

As Regina listened to Agnitio and let his words take root in her head, a sense of purpose began substituting the feeling of helplessness inside of her. She didn't fully grasp yet what Agnitio was saying exactly, but she did feel she had some kind of spark inside of her that was capable of being who she wanted to be. She took a deep breath again and allowed her muscles to relax as she exhaled.

She turned towards her tea, which had changed its color since the last time she looked at it—it was now a sparkling purple. She smiled at the sight of the liquid that resembled an enchanted sky, because she knew the empathetic plant was showing her her own self. She sneaked a smile at Agnitio and drank the Nangrass tea. After the last sparkling drop flowed down her throat, she put the mug down, and noticed that the desperate mood she had entered the hut in was completely gone. Her eyes were awake and open without any sense of tiredness, and she didn't feel like crawling under a blanket to sleep for as long as she could anymore.

"You can't always control what goes on outside," said Agnitio, "but you can always control what goes on inside."

Regina smiled back at the faun, and probably for the first time in her life, she felt like everything was going to be okay.

"Thank you, Agnitio," she thanked the faun again and stood up from the table. "I think . . . It's going to be okay."

"It's going to be just fine," said Agnitio as he stood up as well and looked at Regina with the eyes of a proud parent.

"And it is me who owes you my gratitude."

"For what?" asked Regina with surprise.

"For not leaving," answered Agnitio.

Regina looked at Agnitio with confusion for a couple of seconds then nodded with a smile.

"I'm sure your time is very valuable," she said and stepped aside from the table. "I'll go now. Thank you again."

Brunorth got up from under the chair he could barely fit under anymore, ready to leave with Regina. Regina and the dragon stepped towards the old door and opened it. As her hand was on the doorknob, she turned back to take a last look at Agnitio. He was still standing in the same place with hands placed behind his back, smiling. Regina smiled back and exited the hut.

The person who had walked into the hut a short while ago was not the same person who was stepping out. Regina closed the door behind her, and as she looked at the field in front of her, the green of the grass seemed more vibrant and lively to her than ever before. She even felt a little taller than when she had entered the hut. The soft wind blew her long ash brown hair, so she swept it behind her ears and looked down at Brunorth, who was looking at her joyfully. The dragon had changed so much since they first met. Just like Regina.

She looked at the horizon where the black smudge of Mount Napharata was clearly visible. She rested her eyes on the black piece of sky for a short while then turned towards the huts. People were talking around them, and she saw Joey sitting in front of his, drawing.

As she began walking, the green grass felt soft beneath her feet. Her mouth curved to a smile.

CONTENTS

Made in the USA
Monee, IL
10 February 2020

21572725R00136